PRANK DAY

KEL MITCHELL

WITH MATT MIKALATOS

ILLUSTRATED BY SANTY GUTIÉRREZ

An Imprint of Thomas Nelson

thomasnelson.com

Prank Day

© 2022 Kel Mitchell

Tommy Nelson, PO Box 141000, Nashville, TN 37214

Published in Nashville, Tennessee, by Tommy Nelson. Tommy Nelson is an imprint of Thomas Nelson. Thomas Nelson is a registered trademark of HarperCollins Christian Publishing, Inc.

Tommy Nelson titles may be purchased in bulk for educational, business, fundraising, or sales promotional use. For information, please e-mail SpecialMarkets@ ThomasNelson.com.

Publisher's Note: This novel is a work of fiction. Names, characters, places, and incidents are either products of the author's imagination or used fictitiously. All characters are fictional, and any similarity to people living or dead is purely coincidental.

ISBN 978-1-4002-2924-6 (audiobook)
ISBN 978-1-4002-2923-9 (eBook)
ISBN 978-1-4002-2922-2 (HC)

Library of Congress Cataloging-in-Publication Data
Names: Mitchell, Kel, author. | Mikalatos, Matt, author. | Gutiérrez, Santy, 1971- illustrator.
Title: Prank day / Kel Mitchell with Matt Mikalatos ; illustrated by Santy Gutiérrez.
Description: Nashville, Tennessee : Thomas Nelson, [2022] | Audience: Ages 8-12. | Summary: In an effort to impress Zoe, Chase coordinates a series of practical jokes on the entire town, but when his pranks take on a life of their own, Chase and his friends must search for the culprit.
Identifiers: LCCN 2022007366 (print) | LCCN 2022007367 (ebook) | ISBN 9781400229222 (hardcover) | ISBN 9781400229239 (epub)
Subjects: CYAC: Practical jokes—Fiction. | Middle schools—Fiction. | Schools—Fiction. | Friendship—Fiction. | Humorous stories. | LCGFT: Humorous fiction. | Novels.
Classification: LCC PZ7.1.M633677 Pr 2022 (print) | LCC PZ7.1.M633677 (ebook) | DDC [Fic]—dc23
LC record available at https://lccn.loc.gov/2022007366
LC ebook record available at https://lccn.loc.gov/2022007367

Printed in the United States

22 23 24 25 26   LSC   10 9 8 7 6 5 4 3 2 1

Mfr: LSCC / Crawfordsville, IN / August 2022 / PO #12136508

CONTENTS

For Wisdom and Honor

The entire family loves reading bedtime stories to you both! We all love adding funny voices to the characters and having fun with each page turn (especially me). Well, guess what?! Daddy made his very own action-packed fictional world that we can add to our bedtime story fun vibes! I can't wait to read it to you.

Love you both very much!

DAD

Chapter 1

GET FIT WITH SANTA!

"It's time for me to win Zoe's heart!" the reindeer shouted, straight in Santa's face. It held a flash drive high in one hoof.

"What are you talking about?" Santa asked.

They were standing in a sea of Santas. Hundreds of red-suited figures crowded into the backstage area of the Mitchell View Middle School theater. One Santa had his scraggly white beard caught in a nail on the side of the stage, and two more yanked at his shoulders, to get him unstuck. One Santa rolled back and forth on her backside, trying to get up after falling. But she couldn't get her hands around her enormous pillow belly. Two Santas argued over whether they had switched hats. It was a pandemonium of more-or-less identical Saint Nicks.

"Bobby?" the reindeer asked. "Is that you?"

"I'm Bobby." Another Santa elbowed his way forward and pulled his beard down. "And Chase, you should ditch this plan! You're not cool enough for Zoe, for one thing. Secondly, you're going to give Zoe an 'I love you' video on the last day of school before Christmas break? During the grand finale of the Christmas musical?" Santa Bobby looked at Chase the Reindeer with wide eyes. Bobby had particularly wide eyes, so he often looked surprised. But this time he was doing it on purpose.

Chase the Reindeer pushed his glasses up his nose and held out the flash drive. "This isn't just a video. It's a work of art. Singing. Dancing. Heartfelt professions of love. Three months of work!"

"You hate singing. You're terrible at dancing. And I wrote half the poetry!" Bobby said.

Chase laughed. "Aw, you're my best friend, so what's yours is mine."

"Why give this to her now, Chase? This is the worst possible time!"

"Winter break starts tonight. If I wait, I won't see her for *two whole weeks*."

"SIXTY SECONDS TO CUE!" a man shouted so loudly that half the Santas fell backward. It was Mr. Gino, the theater teacher. Most directors insisted on whispered directions

2

through headphones, or sign language backstage, or at least a blinking countdown sign, but not Mr. Gino. He lived by the old stage adage, "If they don't know who directed this thing, then why do I bother?"

He pointed at Chase. "Reindeer are stage left. STAGE LEFT, CHASE!"

"Right, right, I know," Chase said, backing away from Mr. Gino.

"Left, Chase, LEFT!"

"No problem, Mr. Gino. I just gotta give this to someone real quick."

"FIFTY-FOUR SECONDS!" Mr. Gino bellowed.

Chase grabbed Bobby. "If this all goes right, we're going to get invited to Zoe's famous birthday party. And also, she will be my girlfriend. Wish me luck."

"You're gonna need more than wishes." Bobby pulled his beard back up. Then he paused, looking at Chase's antlers. "Also, it appears that you've dressed as a reindeer of the Svalbard subspecies rather than the breed most commonly assumed to be used by Santa—the Peary caribou."

Chase felt his antlers. "I, uh, just looked at a picture on the internet. Is that a problem?"

"Not at all," Bobby said. "In fact, as an Arctic archipelago, Svalbard seems far more likely to be where the jolly old elf goes for reindeer recruitment. I appreciate your attention to detail and commitment to accuracy, despite the less cinematic nature of the smaller but plucky Svalbard reindeer."

Chase grinned at him. Bobby was always spouting off

random facts. "Hopefully Zoe will be likewise impressed."
Then Chase went wading through the other Santas—most
of them carrying prop gifts or gigantic candy canes—until
he found the one he was looking for. He tapped her on the
shoulder. "Zoe. I'd know you anywhere."

The Santa spun around. "What? I'm not Zoe."

Another Santa pulled her beard down. "I'm over here."

"Ahem." Chase looked down at his black shoes as he
shuffled toward her. "Yes, well. This is for you."

Zoe took the memory stick and looked at it skeptically. "Is
this a Pro-HG memory stick?"

"Uh, yes, and there's a special message *just for you* on it."

Mr. Gino's booming voice came from the audience. "TEN
SECONDS!"

"Just watch it after the show—"

"EIGHT!"

"I have to get ready, Chase." Zoe pulled her beard up.

"SIX!"

Two Santas in sunglasses came up beside them.

"FOUR!"

The cool Santas unzipped their jolly red suits, revealing
Tommy and Timmy Double, or as they liked to be called . . .
the Twinz. Yes, with a Z just like the famous boy band, The
Prank Attackz, whose videos of giant pranks always went viral.

The Twinz modeled their tricks and their outfits on the band. They wore shiny black tracksuits with "Pranks 4 Life" printed on the back and sunglasses. They even styled their hair like one of the band members. Both twins had their hair gelled into a fohawk. They weren't even supposed to be in this show. But here they were, disguised as Santas.

"Yoink!" Tommy, or possibly Timmy, grabbed the memory stick from Zoe. "Go long, bro!"

Chase watched in horror as his artistic tribute to love flew through the air, just like that little baby with wings at Valentine's Day. He didn't know what was about to happen, but he did know this: It would be nothing good.

Chapter 2

A CHEESY LOVE SONG

Chase's memory stick, the one meant for Zoe's eyes only, arced over the crowd of Christmas spectators. All Chase could do was watch. Timmy, or possibly Tommy, caught the pass from his brother and sped for the media booth in the back of the auditorium.

Chase shuddered as the twin ran, all of Chase's private hopes and dreams speeding toward the audiovisual system. "No! That's not for—"

"That's YOUR CUE!" Mr. Gino yelled, and the Santas surged onto the stage like a red tidal wave. Chase tried to fight the current, but he soon found himself pushed to center stage, just a few Santas away from Zoe. If he could just get off the stage, he might have a chance to stop the twin, who was

7

now talking to the sound tech. But the Santas were in tight formation.

"Hey, elves!" Santa Zoe shouted at the top of her lungs.

"Hey!" all the other Santas yelled back.

"We have to get in shape, so we can carry these heavy boxes!"

"Yeah!" The Santas held their props over their heads.

"We're dressed like Santa so we'll sweat it out! And we need all of you"—she pointed at the audience—"to get up and get in shape too!"

The audience jumped to their feet, and Zoe led an aerobic workout to the tune of "Jingle Bells." Three hundred and thirty-three screens around the stage all flashed lyrics with a snowflake bouncing over the words. (Mr. Gino believed if one screen was good, hundreds were incredible.) All of that wouldn't have been *quite* so bad if it had kept going. But it didn't.

The music cut out.

The bouncing snowflakes disappeared.

In their place, three hundred and thirty-three Chases smiled. "Hello, Zoe," the Chase voices said in unison.

The real Chase turned around to hide his face. But the entire back of the stage formed another, gigantic screen. "I know why your feet hurt, girl. Because you've been running

8

through my mind. I can't stop thinking of you, so I wrote you a song called 'Please Be Mine.'"

"Turn it off!" Chase shouted.

"Make it stop!" Bobby groaned.

"Turn it up!" Tommy, or possibly Timmy, whooped, and everyone laughed. Then came Chase's song.

It's not a good experience to discover that you are maybe a little off-key when your love song is being blasted out to your

entire school, all their parents, their grandparents, their little sisters and brothers, and the occasional neighbor. Chase felt his face ignite to one thousand degrees.

The song, now that Chase heard it out loud, was maybe a little cheesy. They had just gotten to the line, "I love you more than a quesadilla, so please be mine." To be fair, he loved quesadillas. A lot.

There was a chance, though, that everyone else hadn't noticed it was cheesy. Maybe they all loved it. Maybe they would think Chase was a genius.

He turned hopefully toward his classmates. Each Santa was howling with laughter. *Okay. Maybe not.*

But there was a chance that Zoe hadn't noticed how lame it was. Maybe *she* loved it. Maybe *she* would think Chase was a genius.

He scanned the crowd of Santas and finally found her . . . doubled over, belly laughing. She was wiping tears out of her eyes, one hand on another Santa's shoulder to keep her balance. If Chase had had a red nose, it would have definitely stopped glowing. A knot grew in his stomach.

"Turn that off!" Mr. Gino shouted, wading through the audience back toward the sound booth. "Turn that off at once and put 'Sweating with Santa' back on!"

But it was too late.

A ragged line of Santas took a bow, and the confused audience members were clapping, laughing, or still trying to do aerobics.

Chase, his head and antlers sagging, snuck out the back door.

"Hey, wait up!" Zoe shouted. She ran to him and gave him a giant hug.

Warmth flooded Chase's body. Maybe . . . maybe the song had actually worked?

"That was the funniest prank I've ever seen," Zoe said. "And I watch The Prank Attackz constantly. That was hilarious, Chase, pretending to be in love with me! Ha! You barely know me. But if I ever did fall in love with someone," she said, "it would be someone who could pull off a giant prank like that."

"Right," Chase said, trying to cover his tracks. "That was a great prank."

"I'm so glad you joined *Get Fit with Santa*. It's cool to be friends."

"Friends," Chase said.

Zoe held out her hand, and Chase shook it stiffly. She smiled, then ran back toward the school. "Merry Christmas, Chase!"

"Merry Christmas," he whispered. He narrowed his eyes and looked at his palm. *Did that count as holding hands?*

11

Probably not. But still, it was cool. Chase sighed. She was *sooo* cute.

A few minutes later Bobby showed up. "That was pretty rough."

"I thought it was funny," Chase said, wiping off his glasses. "A great prank."

"Sure," Bobby said.

"But I can do better."

They started walking home, just one sweaty Santa Claus with his arm around the shoulders of a very sad Svalbard reindeer.

Chapter 3

THE TECHNOLOGY GRAVEYARD

The next day, Chase and Bobby biked to the edge of town, to their favorite place: the Technology Graveyard.

As they rode through a gate, they passed a small mountain of broken record players. Surrounding the pile were the shiny disks that could have played music if any of the players had worked. Nearby there were old-time telephones *with wires*. On the boys' right, the engine of a 1977 Chevy Nova lay in front of one of the original lawnmowers, the machine invented by Edwin Beard Budding in 1830, when his dad handed him a scythe and said, "Time to cut down the grass, Eddie boy." In front of them loomed a computer the size of a house, the old kind that ran on punch cards and electricity.

And here in this strange and beautiful wonderland, you

could buy that giant computer and turn it into a house, if that was something you wanted to do. Because at the Technology Graveyard, strange and outdated inventions of the past could be yours if you could find them and if you were willing to pay the price. And the price was never very much.

Chase had to admit that this was exactly what he needed: a new project to work on with Bobby. His mood was getting better already. There were so many great possibilities here. Just last year, they had discovered a laminator from the 1930s and had used it and some dental laminate to turn every piece of paper in Chase's house into plastic. You could dream big out here.

"What do you boys want?" The owner of the Technology Graveyard, Mrs. Glorka, stepped out of the house near the gate. "Want to sell those bicycles?" Mrs. Glorka was shorter than them and wore thick spectacles and a flowered muumuu. Her hair stood in a beehive almost twice as high as she was tall. She almost never remembered who they were at first, even though they came at least once a month. "She's an alien archaeologist," Bobby whispered, "collecting human technology."

"I'm Chase," Chase said.

"And I'm Bobby," Bobby said.

"And we want to buy some junk," they said together.

"Oh, yes," Mrs. Glorka said. "The weird kid with two arms and the smart kid with one arm."

"Bobby has three arms," Chase corrected her.

Bobby had been born with only his left arm. He had a prosthetic arm, which he was currently wearing. Then he had a third extra-special bionic arm that Chase and Bobby had been building together since first grade. Bobby was currently carrying this creation under his prosthetic arm.

Chase and Bobby had invented the bionic arm using technology they called LIMB: Laudable Incredible Magnificent Boy tech. The arm had a tape player as well as an MP3 player, its own mini speakers, LED lights that flashed to the music's rhythm, a flashlight in one finger, a needle to play records in another, and a portable charger with over fifteen different attachments to allow them to charge all of the old devices they experimented on. That's not even mentioning the forty-seven other features (including a spring-loaded grappling hook).

It was the best arm ever, and Chase was often jealous of it.

"Oh, yes," Mrs. Glorka said. "The weird kid and the kid with three arms. Take your time."

"Thanks, Mrs. Glorka!" They scampered off into the beautiful wilds of discarded equipment.

"Be careful!" Mrs. Glorka yelled after them. "Some of that stuff is dangerous!"

"I laugh at danger," Bobby said, peering into the nozzle of a 1970s blowtorch.

"Me too," Chase said, climbing to the top of a pile of LaserDisc players.

"Ha, ha, ha!" they said together, and grinned at each other.

"Oooooo." Bobby held up a big piece of equipment. "An eight-track player! I bet we could bring this to life again."

But then Chase slumped and slid down the pile in an avalanche of LaserDiscs. He looked off into the distance, his face sappy and sad like some cute puppy on a calendar.

Bobby sighed. "Is this because I said *life* and *Zoe* is the Greek word for *life*?"

Chase's eyes wandered over to his best friend. The look on his face got even sadder, if such a thing were possible. "I didn't even know that, Bobby!"

Just then, a high-pitched beep sounded from a pile of intercom systems. Chase shoved them aside. A faint blue light came from farther beneath.

Bobby put down the eight-track player and picked up an electric hand mixer. "You took your best shot, Chase. And Zoe shook your hand. Let's face it, she's not the kind of girl who wants to pick through garbage. She probably doesn't have the scientific leanings to contribute to the glorious advancement of LIMB technology, either."

Chase frowned. He dug deeper into the pile, like some sort of mole that lived in intercoms instead of in dirt. He reached into the tunnel he had made. Stretching his arm, he felt the warm, rectangular shape of a piece of technology working hard. He just managed to get hold of it with the tips of his fingers, and he pulled it out.

It was a book-sized tablet thing. And it was ancient, at least from the '90s, maybe even the '80s. The words *Palm Pirate* were stamped above the screen. "You're probably right." He pressed a button on the side of the device, and it whirred. "Hey, this thing is booting up!"

"Cool!" Bobby took the Palm Pirate and examined it. "I'm pretty sure my arm has a compatible charger."

"Nice. We're definitely getting this then."

Chase looked off into the distance. "You know . . . we have over three months until April first. And Zoe loves pranks. In fact, she loved my last prank, and I didn't even know it was a prank."

"You don't even like pranks," Bobby said. "Ever since kindergarten when—"

"I know what happened in kindergarten," Chase interrupted. He didn't want to talk about it.

"But we've moved past that, Chase. We're in middle school now."

"Exactly. Maybe I like pranks now," Chase said. The Palm Pirate made a loud whistle sound, and an eight-bit skull face with crossbones appeared on the screen.

"That thing takes a long time to start," Bobby said.

"And maybe I especially like pranks if they can help me get Zoe to be my girlfriend."

"I want the world to be full of hyperintelligent dinosaurs, but I don't see that happening anytime soon."

Chase grabbed the Palm Pirate from Bobby and clicked out the stylus. "Hmmm," He said. "This thing would be perfect for planning things." He wrote on the screen:

```
Plan a series of monster
pranks to win Zoe's heart.
```

The little cartoon skull made a look of surprise. Then it smiled and winked. This thing was great.

Chase studied the words on the Palm Pirate's screen. Then he backspaced and replaced them with the perfect title for his plan:

```
Operation Zoe.
```

Bobby held up the eight-track player. "I'm gonna use this to listen to Grandma's weird old music. She has a pile of eight-track cartridges."

They took their purchases to Mrs. Glorka, who inspected them carefully. She pointed at Bobby. "Don't listen to an eight-track song called 'Muskrat Love.' You'll regret it."

She pointed at Chase. "Be careful. The WF chip is still intact on this Palm Pirate."

"Oh," Chase said. "Right."

Mrs. Glorka looked at them over the top of her spectacles. "You two know what a WF chip is, don't you?"

"Of course we do," they said together.

But they had no idea.

Chapter 4

OPERATION ZOE

"Clowns," Chase muttered. "Spiders, of course. Lions. Googly eyes."

Chase and Bobby were in their secret lair, which wasn't really secret. It also wasn't exactly a lair since it was just Bobby's basement. But it was where they did their best tinkering. Posters of Bobby's favorite movies, including *Tyrannosaurus Rex from the Earth's Core* and *High Velocity Velociraptor*, plastered the walls. There were tools everywhere, several boxes of Christmas decorations, and all of the summer lawn furniture.

"Why clowns?" Bobby asked.

"I know clowns make you nervous," Chase said.

Bobby crossed his arms. "They make any right-thinking person nervous."

"But Tommy, or possibly Timmy, is afraid of them," Chase said. "And it's not enough just to carry out the most epic prank day of all time and win Zoe's heart. I also want to punish the Twinz for pranking me."

"You're not using real clowns, though, are you?"

"Nah, just inflatable dummies dressed as clowns that pop out of the toilets at school."

"That's pretty funny," Bobby admitted. Then he turned his attention back to repairing the eight-track player. He was inserting a new switch system that would let you choose whether to listen to the song at regular speed, one-and-a-half-times speed, three times speed, or—in cases of extreme need—twelve times speed. "So you're going to prank the whole school?"

"Yes, of course," Chase said. "I'm going to—" He wrote on the Palm Pirate:

```
Fill the lunchroom with foam.
Turn the principal's office
       into a fishbowl.
```

"There will be big pranks, small pranks, nice pranks, mean pranks, new pranks, old pranks," Chase continued. "By the end of the day, people won't remember a world without pranks."

"You're going to get kicked out of school."

"Bobby, if I do my job right, I'm going to get kicked out of the whole town. I'm going to prank my parents, my little brother, my neighbors." Chase pushed his glasses back up his nose and wrote on the Pirate. "Which reminds me: I'm going to need some hair clippers."

"Hair clippers?!" Bobby turned to Chase and watched him carefully. "Chase, you have taken this whole thing too far. Once you get to clipping people's hair, the pranks are out of control."

"Who said anything about people?" Chase tapped furiously on the Palm Pirate. "Have I taken on too many pranks? I only have three months to prepare."

Bobby grabbed him by the arms. "Listen to me, Chase. Your obsession with becoming a great prankster has driven you mad. A single prank to get Zoe's attention I can understand. But you're going to prank your parents too? Your neighbors? And what about the Twinz? Tommy can be mean sometimes, but Timmy is actually a nice guy. Or maybe I have that backward; I don't know."

Chase just stared at Bobby's bionic arm. "What if we told everyone your bionic arm had come to life? We could tell them

we onboarded an artificial intelligence and it suddenly has a mind of its own." He continued writing.

```
Bring Bobby's bionic arm to life.
```

"It's too much, Chase! You're going too far. There will be consequences—I can feel it! Haven't you ever watched a single movie or read any books? Mad scientists' creations always get away from them. Pranksters always end up getting pranked by their own elaborate tricks."

Chase stood up and walked to the far wall to stare out the window. It wasn't an actual window, of course. They were in the basement. It was a picture of a window painted on the wall. But Chase liked to pretend he could look outside while he did his best thinking. Chase stood and looked over the fake beach, where fake waves stood frozen under fake seagulls. "Don't you see, Bobby? I would do anything for Zoe. I would prank more than my family, more than my neighbors, more than the entire school. I would prank animals. I would prank everything on the planet. Yes, Bobby, I would prank the entire world if that's what it would take to make Zoe fall in love with me. When I'm done, these pranks will make me the coolest kid in school. In fact, I'm putting that on my list!"

Chase scribbled furiously onto the Palm Pirate, which whirred and dinged and flashed bright lights as he wrote.

```
Become coolest kid in school.
```

"You're making a mistake," Bobby said sadly. "And I don't want any part in it."

Chase turned from the fake window. "You're not going to help me?"

Bobby shook his head. "Chase, I'm your best friend. I know you better than anyone. You're pretending to be someone you aren't. I'll remind you again, *you don't even like pranks*."

"But I do like Zoe."

"That reminds me of an old saying: 'For what doth it profit a prankster if he gaineth a girlfriend but loseth his soul?'"

Chase narrowed his eyes. "I don't think that's a real saying."

"Well, something like that."

"Bah!" Chase said and held up the Palm Pirate so Bobby could see the long to-do list on the screen. "I'll do it all myself then! I will be the greatest prankster of all time, and no one will share my glory! *Moowhahahahahaaaaaaa!*"

And he stormed up the stairs, slammed the basement door, politely said goodnight to Bobby's Grandma Agnus, ran home, said hi to his parents, gave his little brother, Drake, a hug, stormed up his stairs, and

slammed his door. Then he remembered he had forgotten the Palm Pirate, went back downstairs and over to Bobby's, knocked on the door, went inside, went to the basement, grabbed the Palm Pirate, and stormed up the stairs again.

After Chase had left again, Bobby reached into a pile of eight-tracks on his grandmother's bookshelf. He put the eight-track for "Muskrat Love" into his newly repaired machine. "I have a bad feeling about this," he said to no one in particular as the music began.

"Hey, Mrs. Glorka was right. This song is terrible!" He turned the speed to twelve times normal speed and let the music burst past him.

Chapter 5

PRANK DAY

January: Chase gathered materials, and he spent every free moment in his room writing feverishly on the Palm Pirate. One evening, his mom brought him a quesadilla. "Working hard on your homework, hon?" He was home, and he was working, that much was true.

"I can't be distracted now, Mom. I'm busy!"

"But it's a quesadilla," she said. "Your favorite."

"Just leave it," he snapped. He felt bad later, but a prank genius needs to concentrate.

February: Chase's dad checked on him increasingly often, his eyes wide at the charts and schematics littering the walls of Chase's room. "Quite a plan you got there, son." Chase looked up from his work, bleary-eyed. *But would it be enough?* That was the question.

His dad punched him playfully in the arm. "When I was a kid, I taped a sign on my old man's back. Pranks! Ha!" *Yes,* Chase thought. *Yes, of course. Signs . . . a classic old-school prank.* He wrote it on the Palm Pirate:

```
A sign for Dad.
```

"I'm worried about you, son," his dad said. "You're getting distant from the family. You don't even seem to be having fun making these pranks."

"I know," Chase said, not really listening. "It's so fun, right?"

March: Chase's little brother, Drake, peeked in. "All this for a girl, huh?" Chase looked up from the drone he was currently modifying. Six of the eight legs worked correctly now. Could he finish before the rapidly approaching deadline of April first? Chase took his glasses off and rubbed his weary eyes.

"Not 'a girl,' Drake. We're talking about Zoe. The greatest woman to ever live."

"Uh-huh," Drake said. "Well, maybe it's different in middle school, but in grade school, I find that women just want to be appreciated and treated with respect."

Chase rolled his eyes. "You'll know better when you're a little older."

Finally, the turning pages of the calendar led to . . .

April first. At last.

Chase opened his eyes moments before the alarm went off. "This is it!" He jumped out of bed. "Operation Zoe starts now."

Chase ran to the mirror. He had taped a picture of Zzak from The Prank Attackz on the edge. On a normal day, Chase had natural, long, kinky hair. He usually used a curl sponge

and leave-in conditioner spray to get the curly coils that were his look. But not today.

Chase set a small case in front of the mirror and opened it slowly and respectfully. Inside were gold barber trimmers. These were his dad's pride and joy. Chase had snuck them out last night.

He switched the trimmers on and grinned at the buzzing in his hand. "Frohawk coming up," he said. Then he carefully faded the sides of his hair with a cool design on each side. "Looking sharp." He nodded at himself in the mirror.

"Not done yet though," he said. "You handsome, handsome man." He curled his hair with the sponge. "Perfect."

Chase took off his glasses and squinted into the mirror. *Hmmm.* His vision wasn't *too* fuzzy. But something was missing. Ah, yes. The black track jacket. Now he looked exactly right. He slipped his glasses into the jacket pocket.

Downstairs, he poured a bowl of cereal. Drake was eating oatmeal. "Hey, baby bro, can you get me some milk?"

"You better not have used Dad's clippers," Drake said, looking at Chase's hair. "You know that thing is his baby."

"Don't tell Dad, and I'll cut your hair later." He winked at his little brother. "Now how about that milk?"

"Sure!" Drake opened the refrigerator door and screamed. Chase had put googly eyes on everything in there. "The fruit

31

has eyes!" Drake shouted. "Mom! Dad! Help!"

Chase wrapped his arms around Drake. "Mom and Dad have disappeared," he said, and Drake ran out of the room screaming.

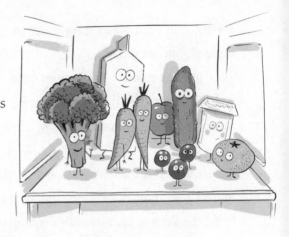

Chase snickered to himself as he grabbed his backpack. "I'm just getting warmed up."

On the way toward the door, he stopped by the hallway bathroom. His mom was standing in front of the mirror, her hair wet, a hair dryer in one hand. Chase tried to hide his laughter. "Hey, Mom, I'm headed to school!"

"Okay, son, have fun!" She turned on the hair dryer, and a swirling poof of white flour covered her face and hair. "*Chase!* Did you put flour in my hair dryer?"

"Don't worry, Mom. It's a new look that's all the rage!"

Drake came screaming down the hallway. He took one look at Mom and shouted, "Mom is a ghost!" and ran back the other way.

This is going great, Chase thought, and he popped out the front door. His dad was outside, about to get in his car.

"Hey there, son! Is that a new look?"

"Hey, Dad! Yeah, trying something new. How do you like it?"

"If you like it, son, I love it." His dad paused. "To get that fade just right, we should use my clippers. I'll run and get them and clean you up."

"Uh, no, Dad, no. You gotta get to work."

"Okay," Dad said. "Maybe tonight." As his dad got in the car, Chase snuck around back and stuck a sign to the trunk: "Honk. My Dad Doesn't Know It's April Fools' Day."

Chase turned his bike down the street and grinned as he heard the chorus of car horns starting.

Zoe was going to love his pranks. And these were just the warm-ups. The next prank was an epic one, the kind of prank that in an ordinary year would be considered a best-of-year classic. He set his bike down, pulled the clippers out of his bag, and jumped the neighbor's fence.

Mr. and Mrs. Nutmeg were nice enough neighbors, even if they walked around the neighborhood in spandex jogging suits all day. Their first jaunt of the morning usually ended just after Chase left for school. And since he had left early today, that should mean he had enough time to visit their dog, Fluffy.

Chase grinned to himself and crossed into their yard. He reached into his bag and pulled out the gold clippers. "I have got a special treat for you today, Fluffy. You're about to get the clipping of a lifetime." Fluffy looked up at him with big brown eyes as the clippers buzzed.

He had just finished his work of art when Mr. Nutmeg opened the back door and called for his pet. Chase crouched behind the doghouse, snickering. Fluffy bounced up to Mr. Nutmeg, who cried out and yelled for his wife. "Someone has turned our beautiful dog into a lion!" Chase grinned. It had taken some creative trimming, but he had given Fluffy a giant mane and one big fluff ball on the end of his tail.

But there was no time to hang out and enjoy the screams of his neighbors. Chase needed to move on to see the other pranks he had planted go off. He had decorated Principal Meyer's office in a Very Special Way. There were the bathrooms at school, which would be opening soon. And he needed to buzz by the football field. Then, of course, there was the school lunchroom.

But first he needed to stop by and pick up Bobby.

He skidded to a stop outside Bobby's house and rapped on the front door. Grandma Agnus answered. "Chase? Bobby said you weren't riding to school together today."

"He did?"

"Something about being worried you'd prank him."

Chase frowned. "I'd never prank Bobby. He's my best friend." He leaned close. "But Grandma Agnus, there's something you should know: we've been experimenting on Bobby's bionic arm, and I'm afraid that it has become self-aware."

Grandma Agnus looked at him carefully. "Is that so?"

"Yeah. So be careful!"

Grandma Agnus looked behind her, and Chase jumped on his bike.

He was just getting started.

Chapter 6

BUSTED!

Building the drone was the easy part.

Decorating it to look like a spider—a very convincing, giant black spider with eight terrible legs and shiny eyes that could stare into your very soul—had taken several weeks of his March. But watching it take flight over the football field was worth all the work.

Chase didn't like pranks. But standing under the bleachers with the remote control, sending that flying spider swooping over the terrified football players as they broke formation, made Chase think he could learn to love them. One of the Twinz fell as he ran, and Chase gleefully made the spider drone dive down over him. In the middle of the field, Coach Buckets was screaming at the team to focus, his face hot-tamale red.

Chase laughed so hard that tears streamed down his cheeks. But he had to hurry to the lunchroom. The morning bell was about to ring. He put the remote control in his backpack and sprinted to the cafeteria. As students milled around waiting for class to start, Chase quietly opened a lunchroom window and motioned to a man in overalls who was holding a giant hose.

"You sure this is what you want to do, kid?" the guy asked.

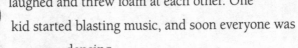

Chase folded up a ten-dollar bill and put it in the man's shirt pocket, just like he had seen in his favorite cartoon mafia movie, *The Codfather*. "I think this should make my intentions clear."

The man shrugged and turned on his machine. A gigantic blast of foam sprayed into the lunchroom. Kids slipped and fell as they laughed and threw foam at each other. One kid started blasting music, and soon everyone was dancing.

Chase nodded. "My work here is done." The bell for class rang, and Chase quickly grabbed a special box from his locker and raced to his first class.

He raised his hand immediately. "Mrs. Handler? Mrs. Handler? I have a special treat for the class. Caramel apples!" He opened the box, and everyone cheered.

"Wait," Mrs. Handler said. "There have been a lot of mysterious pranks going on today. I heard the office has been vandalized."

"Someone put fake clowns in all the toilets," a girl said.

One of the Twinz shuddered. "Inflatable mannequins dressed like clowns! When you walk into the stall, they pop out of the toilets! My brother had to go to the nurse's office to recover. He's so scared of clowns."

"Foam in the lunchroom!"

"A flying spider!"

"My shoelaces were tied together!"

Chase raised an eyebrow. That last one wasn't his prank. He was a professional, not some opportunistic, fly-by-the-seat-of-your-pants amateur.

"So," Mrs. Handler said, "I just want to make sure this isn't a prank."

"Oh sure," Chase said, and he chose a specially prepared caramel-covered surprise for himself. He took a big bite and showed the apple to the class. "Nothing but one hundred percent delicious caramel treat."

The other kids swarmed Chase. Each one took a caramel-covered snack and started munching.

"Gross!"

"This is disgusting!"

One girl, Franchesca, stared down at the golden snack as her fingers fidgeted with a flower patch on her jeans. She also had a fabric flower in her dark-brown hair. She was a bit of a hippie and liked to talk about world peace, but she didn't look peaceful now. "Is this a caramel-covered"—she felt her face—"*onion*?!"

Chase laughed, pleased they had all fallen for it. "As a matter of fact, it is!"

"But I'm allergic," Franchesca said, sweat pouring down her face. She reached toward her backpack. "My . . . Epi . . . Pen."

Franchesca's head started to swell like an inflating balloon. The other kids screamed.

"She's gonna pop!" one of the kids yelled.

This was not good. Chase

raced to Franchesca's backpack and spilled it out on the floor. Her head *did* look like a balloon. If it popped, he wouldn't be remembered as the greatest prankster of all time; he would be remembered as the guy who blew up Franchesca.

"It's gotta be here . . ."

And then he found it. He snatched up the EpiPen and handed it to Franchesca. She popped the cap off and stabbed herself. Immediately the swelling went down.

"I'm going to be okay," she said.

"My bad," Chase said sheepishly.

But as Franchesca's giant head shrank, Chase saw Mrs. Handler standing behind her. Her arms were crossed, her foot tapped, and a giant scowl covered her face.

Just as Mrs. Handler opened her mouth to reprimand Chase, the classroom speaker crackled to life. Principal Meyer's voice echoed out. "One of you students has been terrorizing the school with your April Fools' pranks. These shenanigans must stop now! The next prank I hear about, that student will get Saturday detention. Never in the history of Mitchell View Middle School have we seen a rash of pranks so enormous, and I promise you . . . you will pay!"

"Ahem," Chase said. "I think I hear my cell phone ringing." He pulled out his phone. It wasn't ringing, but he put it up to his ear. "Oh, hi, Mom. I have a dentist appointment and should ride home immediately? Okay, bye."

But Mrs. Handler was still glaring at him.

"Principal's office?" he asked.

"Principal's office," she agreed.

Chase gulped, packed his bag, and started walking.

Chapter 7

CHASE IS IN OVER HIS HEAD

Chase stood in front of the principal's door, taking deep breaths. "This will be fine," he said to himself. "What's the worst that can happen"

The door flew open, and Principal Meyer pointed at a chair in front of her desk. She did not look happy. In fact, she looked unhappy. In fact, she looked like she had been unhappy once upon a time and it was a fond memory of better days.

"Chase," she said. "Sit."

Principal Meyer's office looked like a giant diorama of the ocean. A thick layer of sand blanketed the floor, pieces of coral covered her desk, and pictures of fish swam over the walls. In the center of her desk was a giant bowl with hundreds of goldfish inside.

"Nice place you got here," Chase said, doing his best to sound upbeat.

"When I came in this morning," Principal Meyer said, "there were three hundred and twenty-two paper cups filled with water on the floor. And each one held a goldfish."

"Actually," Chase said, "I miscounted. There was one cup with two fish."

"Listen, Chase, everyone likes you—"

Chase sat up straighter. "They do?! If everyone likes me, then you must be saying . . . I'm the most popular kid in the school!"

"—but that's not going to save you here."

His plan was working! He was the coolest kid around. And Zoe was sure to notice. He remembered the touch of her hand on his.

Principal Meyer was prattling on. "No excuse . . . Saturday detention . . . kicked out of school."

Chase's eyes flew wide. "Principal Meyer! You can't kick me out of school. My parents will ground me for life!"

"Well," she said, "you should have thought of that before you put three hundred and twenty-two cups and three hundred and twenty-three fish in my office, foamed the lunchroom, and scared the Twinz half to death with clowns and a flying spider. Why, both of them have been in the nurse's office crying. Even the nice one!"

Chase shook his head. "I just came from class, ma'am, and one of the Twinz was in there."

Principal Meyer shrugged. "Aw, you've seen one, you've seen them both. The point, Chase, is that I'm going to kick you out of school."

"You don't understand! My parents will actually ground me for life. I'll have to get a job I can do from my room. If I get married, my wife will have to move into the house. I'll never feel the fresh air on my face again."

Just then, the door flung open to reveal . . . Mr. Gino, the theater teacher! That guy sure knew how to make an entrance.

"Oh, don't be so dramatic, Chase!" he said dramatically.

Mr. Gino was everyone's favorite teacher. Bobby and Chase had agreed to be in the Christmas play just so they could hang with him. He liked to have every student in his productions. *"Everyone has a part to play, because everyone has a part,"* he always liked to say.

Principal Meyer's whole face lit up. "Eugene!"

Chase said it to himself quietly, just to make sure he had heard that correctly: "Eugene Gino."

"That's right," Mr. Gino said. "And I've come to say that Chase is a great kid. This isn't like him at all. Why, just look at the way he's dressed, Maya!"

Maya Meyer?!

Principal Meyer looked at Chase carefully. "You're right. Why, Chase is usually a quiet enough boy with glasses. But now he's got a frohawk, has ditched his glasses, and is wearing a shiny jacket."

"It can mean only one thing," Mr. Gino said.

"He's joined a gang!" Principal Meyer exclaimed.

Mr. Gino shook his head. "He's in *love*."

Principal Meyer gasped.

"It's more of a crush," Chase said sheepishly.

"Ohhhh, pranks for love," Principal Meyer said, batting her eyelashes at Mr. Gino. "That makes more sense."

"Uh, pranks for a crush," Chase said. "Let's not get ahead of ourselves."

"If it's for *love*," Principal Meyer said, "I guess I won't kick him out of school completely."

"Oh yeah, pranks for love," Chase said. "Deep love. Definitely love."

Mr. Gino studied the fishbowl on the principal's desk. "I have an idea. Why don't you put him in charge of cleaning everything up?"

"Great idea," Principal Meyer and Chase said together.

"Also . . . Chase is really great with old technology. Just last week he helped me turn on the air conditioner in my classroom. Two weeks ago he got my overhead projector running again. And it just so happens I need someone who can use ancient equipment to run tech for my next theater production."

"Deal," Chase said.

"Hmmm," Principal Meyer said. "It's a good plan. But I think he should get Saturday detention too."

Chase sagged in his chair. "Okay."

Mr. Gino clapped him on the shoulder. "Come on, pal. I'll get you started cleaning in the lunchroom."

Principal Meyer jumped up a little too quickly. She came over to Mr. Gino and got so close that he had to lean backward and put his hand on the wall to keep his balance. "Wonderful," Principal Meyer said. "I'll let you handsome—uh, I mean, *handle* that."

Chase pushed the door open. "Ugh, someone give me a mop. I want to get to work right away."

Mr. Gino walked alongside him, a grin on his face. "So you're going to run tech for my next theatrical masterpiece, *The Glove Diaries*."

"I guess. What's it about?"

"I'm still working on that," he said as he led Chase to the janitor's closet.

Chapter 8

THE BEST APRIL FOOLS' DAY EVER

If Chase had to guess how much foam was in the lunchroom, he would peg it at right around seven tons. He knew immediately that cleaning it all with a single mop would take somewhere between forever and eternity. So he set out to find a technological solution.

As soon as Mr. Gino left, he inspected the janitor's closet. The ancient industrial vacuum cleaner looked promising. This gigantic metal monstrosity was designed for cleaning the more robust dirt of the 1960s. When Chase plugged it in, the machine made a sound like a jet engine.

The floors were so slippery that the vacuum moved like a ballet dancer on ice. Next, he attached a folding chair with two bungee cords. Then he rode the vacuum cleaner in zigzags across the lunchroom. The machine sucked up foam as Chase shouted from underneath his mop-bucket helmet (safety first!) and steered with the mop.

Sure, no one had said he could use the giant vacuum cleaner. But he didn't think it would get him in any more trouble. He was killing it at a new game he called "Foam Rider Extreme: Chase Style" when a familiar voice called his name.

"Huh?" Chase took the bucket off his head and switched off his Foam Rider. He looked around and found . . . Zoe! "Uh. Hey, Zoe, are you lost or something?"

Zoe laughed, and the sound flowed through his body like the feeling of eating something cold on a hot day. "I go to school here, don't I? I'm not lost. I'm looking for *you*."

Chase looked behind him. Maybe she was talking to some other guy. But he was the only other person in the room. *Think, Chase, what can you do to make sure that the nicest, friendliest, prettiest, smartest, nicest, friendliest, prettiest, smartest, nicest*—uh-oh, he was caught in a loop and . . . What was he supposed to be doing again? Oh yeah! Impress Zoe. But now she was just watching him with her eyebrows raised. He didn't have any more time to think of a solution, so . . .

He tried to do a fancy dismount from the Foam Rider, but he slipped in the foam and landed on his side. Still trying to recover, he rested his chin on his hand and racked his brain for something fancy to do. Like . . . a French accent! *"Oui, mademoiselle*, how can *moi* be of service?"

Zoe's eyes lit up and she laughed. "I thought you were in Spanish class."

"Uh. *Sí.* I am. But . . ." *How does she know that?* She had always been nice to him and Bobby, but . . . *Wait, what is she doing in here talking to me again?* He looked around for a clue. "Do you need me to clean up the clowns in the bathroom or something?"

"Ha! I love those clowns. Everyone's talking about your pranks, and I've been laughing all morning."

His plan was working!

"I'm having a big party tomorrow," Zoe continued. "And I wanted to invite you."

Chase started to answer, but his brain, already struggling, shut down from the shock. "Uuuuuuuh."

She smiled. "I'll help you. Take out your phone."

He took it out.

"Now put it in my hand."

He did.

She put her number in and handed the phone back. "Now call me so I have your number."

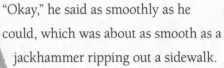

"Uh-huh." He dialed, and Zoe's phone started ringing.

She pressed Answer and looked him in the eyes. "Hi, Chase. See you at my place tomorrow."

"Okay," he said as smoothly as he could, which was about as smooth as a jackhammer ripping out a sidewalk. "O—k—k—k—k-aaaaay."

Zoe winked at him and walked out.

Chase put the bucket back on his head and grabbed the mop. The mop was an electric guitar. It was a javelin! It was a pole for vaulting!

He was in mid-victory dance when he heard Zoe's voice again. Chase froze.

"Oh yeah. And wear that jacket tomorrow. I really like it."
Then she was gone again. Chase left the Foam Rider in the
middle of the lunchroom and followed her into the hall. He
needed to find Bobby.

Bobby was in the library, reading *A Brief History of Clowns*.

"Looks interesting," Chase said.

Bobby glanced up. "My counselor says that if there's
something that upsets you, it's good to research that thing." He
looked at the book. "It's more interesting than pranks, that's
for sure."

"Aw, Bobby. I'm sorry I made you feel left out. But
Operation Zoe worked! We got invited to the party tomorrow
night!"

Bobby stopped in the middle of a page turn. "You're joking."

"She loved the pranks. And now that we're in, we never
have to do another prank again. We can go back to fixing old
tech and learning about clowns or whatever we want."

"I can't believe it," Bobby said, shaking his head. "And you
didn't get in trouble with the school, even."

"Welllll . . . I have to run tech for Mr. Gino's next play, *The
Glove Diaries*. And I have Saturday detention tomorrow."

"What?! You think your parents are going to let you go to a
party if you have detention?!"

Chase's heart sank. "Oh no, Bobby. I didn't even think of

that. And Principal Meyer always sends an email! They'll read about it tonight."

Bobby clapped him on the back. "Don't worry, pal. I'll come over for a sleepover. We'll play online games and use so much bandwidth that your parents' email won't even load."

And that is exactly what they did.

Except for one more thing.

That night they sat at Chase's desk, where the Palm Pirate was humming along and shooting out strange sparks of light. Bobby got a funny little smile on his face and said, "You know, I wish I had done a couple of pranks with you. Just some of the classics. Like prank phone calls."

Chase grinned. "It's not too late."

He picked up his phone. "This has been the best April Fools' Day ever. I wish it would never end."

"Me too," Bobby said, grinning. "Call Mr. Gino first!"

Chase dialed Mr. Gino's number. He dropped his voice lower and said, "Excuse me, sir. Is your refrigerator running? . . . Then you better go catch it!" He hung up and they both laughed hysterically.

"My turn, my turn," Bobby said. "Let's call Principal Meyer . . . Hello, miss. May I speak to the walls . . . Wrong number? Do you mean to say there are no walls there? Then how does the roof stay up?"

When they had stopped laughing, the boys turned out the lights.

"Good night, Bobby."

"Good night, Chase."

"I wish every day was April Fools'," Chase said.

"But then we couldn't go to Zoe's party," Bobby said.

Chase smiled. "Yeah. That's true. Maybe tomorrow will be an even better day than today."

They fell asleep, with the only light in the room the occasional spark from the Palm Pirate.

Chapter 9

THE FRIENDLY LION

"That's not funny, Chase," Bobby said the next morning, sitting straight up in bed.

Chase put his glasses on. "What?"

"Taking my *arm*."

Chase gasped. "What? I would never!"

But Bobby was already headed out the door, grumbling to himself.

Chase jumped up. "Bobby, I promised never to prank you, and I never will!"

"Whatever, Chase. I have to go home and get my other arm. Unless you want to give me the bionic one back."

"I didn't take it; I promise."

After Bobby left, Chase ran down the stairs. He needed to

eat some breakfast and get off to detention before his parents asked any questions. The last thing he needed was to have to explain why he couldn't do some extra chore because he needed to get to detention on time.

He put his hand on the refrigerator door.

"I wouldn't do that if I were you." Drake was sitting at the counter, eating cereal.

"Why not?"

"They don't like it."

"Who doesn't like it?"

"*Them.* You know. I know you know."

But Chase didn't know. "I'm gonna just grab an apple to eat really quick." He popped the door open and grabbed an apple.

"CLOSE THE DOOR!"

"KNOCK IT OFF. IT'S TOO BRIGHT!"

"MY EYES, MY EYES!"

Chase slammed the door again. "Hey, Drake?"

"Yeah?"

"Was that a whole bunch of talking fruits and vegetables?"

"They have eyes too."

Chase looked at the apple in his hand. It opened its eyes. "Please don't eat me. I have a wife and forty children."

Chase dropped the apple.

"OUCH!" It rolled under the table.

Drake shook his head. "That apple was lying. It can't have children before you eat it. All the seeds are inside."

Chase stared at Drake. "Why are you so calm?"

"Fool me once, shame on you. Fool me twice, shame on me." Drake glared at him and took another bite of cereal.

"I have nothing to do with this!" Chase said.

"Uh-huh."

"I have to go," Chase said. "And I'm skipping breakfast."

As he pushed his bike onto the sidewalk, he noticed a strange sight: a black sedan with tinted windows sat in front of Mr. and Mrs. Nutmeg's house. "That's weird." He snuck up to the neighbors' front door and peeked through the window.

Mr. and Mrs. Nutmeg were crying, and a man in a black suit and sunglasses was watching them. "He ate my little Fluffy!" Mrs. Nutmeg was saying. The man wasn't trying to comfort her. And he wasn't saying anything. He was just watching.

Ate Fluffy? Who would do that? Chase jumped the fence and bent over to look into Fluffy's doghouse.

Two bright, feline eyes stared back. Very large feline eyes.

A lion stepped out of the doghouse. "Whoa!" Chase hopped backward.

The lion jumped up, put its paws on Chase's shoulders, and licked his face. "Ew, gross! Stop that." He pushed the lion away. Then a terrible thought came to him. He pointed his finger at the lion and said, "Sit!"

The lion sat down immediately.

"Shake! Roll over! Play dead!"

The lion did it all.

"Fluffy, is that you?" He could have sworn the lion was grinning at him.

Chase couldn't deal with this. He was going to be late for detention. He jumped on his bike and raced to school. He burst into detention right on time, panting from running up the stairs. The bored teacher was doing a crossword puzzle, and the bored kids were staring at the walls.

Chase walked to the window, still stunned by the new Fluffy.

"Sit down," the teacher said without looking up from her crossword puzzle.

Chase took a step away from the window, but a movement caught his eye. Down below, something was sprinting across the parking lot. Something big and blocky and white. Something big and blocky and white and wearing sneakers and also a sweatband. Chase cleared his throat. "Um. There's a refrigerator jogging around down there."

"April Fools' was yesterday," one of the kids said.

"Yeah. Good try, Chase."

The teacher crossed to the window, looked down, and let out a yelp. "Class dismissed!"

"What?!" All the kids jumped up and ran to the window.

The teacher was already headed out the door. "I'm gonna get video of this. I'll make enough money to never teach again! Ha, ha, ha! I'm gonna be rich!"

"I guess we can go home then," one student said.

Chase continued to stare out the window. The apple. Fluffy. The refrigerator. What was going on? Then he remembered Bobby. *Oh no. What had happened to Bobby's arm?*

He dashed down the stairs toward his bike.

Chapter 10

SOME DISARMING NEWS

It felt like something was rolling around in Chase's stomach. Good thing he hadn't eaten that angry apple. He thought back to the moment that Bobby had left his house this morning. Bobby was mad about his missing arm. And with the fruit and the lion and the refrigerator, Chase was starting to get worried.

As he biked down the street, he noticed a black sedan driving slowly through the neighborhood. It was just like the one that had been parked in front of Mr. and Mrs. Nutmeg's house.

Suddenly, a shape jumped out of the bushes and tackled Chase to the ground. Chase struggled, but the stranger was too strong. Chase swung his arms wildly as he was dragged into the bushes.

"Chase! Knock it off. It's me, Bobby!"

Chase knocked it off, and it actually was Bobby. "What's the big idea, tackling me into the bushes?"

Bobby shushed Chase and looked back toward his house. He watched for a moment before he turned back to Chase. "Listen. This morning I left your house to go get my other arm."

"Yeah, I know, and I can see you have your 'everyday' arm on right now."

"*Shhh!* So when I got home, there were two people in black suits waiting for me inside."

A chill went down Chase's back. "I saw those people at Mr. and Mrs. Nutmeg's house. I think they might be animal control."

"They're not with animal control. It's even worse."

"Worse than animal control?! Is it the Department of Sanitation? Public utilities inspectors?"

Bobby shook his head gravely. "You'll never guess. I'd never heard of their department before." A business card appeared between his fingers, and he flipped it to Chase.

"Uh," Chase said. "This is blank."

"Exactly, Chase, exactly. They're so top secret they don't put anything on their business cards."

"Then why do they even have business cards?"

"Because they have money to burn—an unlimited budget! They have government funds and the freedom to do whatever they want. And they're asking about *your pranks*, Chase."

Chase gasped. "But why?"

"So here's the rest of the story," Bobby said. "The agents wanted to know if I had seen anything weird. I said, 'Weird, like what?' Then they looked at each other before one of them said, 'Lions in the street, that sort of thing.' So I thought they were talking about your pranks yesterday. I said, 'Oh, those were just pranks.' And they said, 'We assure you this is very serious, young man.' Then I heard this weird snapping."

"Snapping?" Chase leaned closer. "What kind of snapping?"

"Like someone snapping their fingers. In fact, exactly like that. I looked down the hallway and there was my bionic arm, trying to get my attention."

A chill went down Chase's spine. "What do you mean 'trying to get your attention'?"

"It was in the hallway, standing on its end—the part that attaches at my elbow. When I looked at it, it pointed at the ceiling. Or that's what I thought at first. Then I realized it was holding up one finger to shush me."

"Your arm."

"Yes."

"Was shushing you."

"Exactly. So as soon as I could sneak away, I texted Mr. Gino and told him we needed help. We have to get you away from these agents. I'm going to stick around here and see if I can figure out exactly what's going on."

As if on cue, Mr. Gino rolled up in his 1970 Chevy Chevelle SS convertible with the top down. "Hello? Anyone here?" Mr. Gino slowed the car and looked all around. "Bobby? You said to meet you by the bushes in front of your house, but all I see is this abandoned bicycle."

The boys leapt out of the bushes, and Bobby pushed Chase into the front seat. There were a bunch of boxes in the back, so Bobby grabbed Chase's bike and stuffed it in the trunk.

"That kid's been working out," Mr. Gino said.

"Mr. Gino," Bobby said. "There are some weird bad guys after Chase, and I need you to help him hide for a few hours while we figure out what to do."

Mr. Gino chuckled. "Well, why didn't you say so already, my man? I'll take care of it. I was in similar trouble when I was in middle school. What had happened was—"

The door to Bobby's house flew open, and two men in black suits and sunglasses rushed to the curb. "There he is!"

"Great story, Mr. Gino," Bobby said. "But you gotta go!"

"Burn rubber!" Chase shouted as the two government agents rushed toward the Chevelle.

"Who were those guys?" Mr. Gino asked as he hit the gas. "Animal control?"

"Even worse," Chase replied. He looked in the rearview mirror and watched his best friend's image grow smaller as they rocketed away. "Even worse."

Chapter 11

THE POISON APPLE

The car pulled in to Lyle's Village Pantry and parked by the gas pump.

Chase got out. "I'm going to get a soda."

"Be careful," Mr. Gino said as he put gas in the tank. "I think we lost those guys, but my awesome car is really easy to notice."

Chase nodded, then walked into the shop. If you needed to buy something, Lyle's Village Pantry had it: snacks, drinks, ice cream, microwave meals, air fresheners, toilet paper, stuffed animals, headphones, matches, luggage, backpacks, mosquito spray, fire extinguishers, fireworks, chocolate coins, pet mice, pet cats, replacement screen doors, and new tires.

"Hi, Chase," Lisa said from behind the checkout counter.

The place was called Lyle's Village Pantry, but Chase had

never met Lyle. Lisa was a skinny teenager with a big poofed hairdo, and she always seemed to be working. "We've got some new snacks today," Lisa said. "You want the rundown?"

"I just want a soda," Chase said.

"Sodas are between the ketchup and the mouse pads."

"Thanks."

There were about seventeen brands of soda at Lyle's, but Chase loved Chivalry, the plum-flavored soda. Put it together with some Oishi potato chips and you had a real taste sensation. He grabbed a cold Chivalry and was headed to the counter when someone tapped him on the shoulder.

He whirled around expecting to see a stone-faced government agent, but instead it was . . . Franchesca. From school.

"Hi, it's me, Franchesca," she said. "From school?"

What a relief! "Franchesca, hi! I'm really sorry about yesterday. It was just an April Fools' joke gone horribly wrong. I had no idea you were allergic to onions. I didn't even know that was a thing!"

"It's okay. I'm fine now. You just buying a soda?"

"Yup. Hey, do you think there are people in the world who are allergic to broccoli? And do you think I could convince my mom that I'm one of them?"

Lisa wandered over with a big tray of snacks. "Hi, Franchesca. Here are the snacks we just started serving today."

Franchesca's eyes lit up. "I always like to see the new snacks. What have you got?"

"We have broiled crickets, of course. Astronaut ice cream—that's actually pretty good. And our new favorite: delicious, sweet, juicy caramel-covered onions."

Panic filled Chase's throat. How close did Franchesca have to get to an onion before she turned into an overinflated blimp? A picture of her giant head yesterday popped into Chase's mind. This was his chance to make up for his mistake and save Franchesca's life!

"Don't mind if I do," Franchesca said, and picked up a caramel-covered onion.

Chase leapt in the air like a basketball champ, lifted his hand high, and slapped the onion so hard that it pinwheeled across the market and splattered into the automatic door. It slid down the glass, leaving a shiny trail of brown sugar all the way to the floor. "She's allergic to onions!"

Franchesca smiled at him and picked up another onion. "Not anymore. These are one hundred percent delicious. You should try one." She took a big bite. *Crunch!* She chewed happily, smiling the whole time. Then she held the half-eaten onion out to Chase.

"Um. No thanks."

Lisa cocked her head and looked at Chase. "Are you okay? You're acting really weird."

Chase grabbed Franchesca by the arm and yanked her outside.

"Chase, what is going on?" she asked.

He looked all around him, then leaned close. "I did a bunch of pranks yesterday, and they are all coming true today. Like when I said caramel-covered onions are delicious. Evidently now they are."

Franchesca took another big bite. *Cr-runch!* "I'm allergic to apples now, which is too bad. But then again, when my mom tried to cut one up today, it yelled at her. But I can eat all the onions I want! That's pretty cool."

"No, it's not cool!" Chase paced in front of the store, waving his arms. "I turned a dog into a lion! Fruit can talk! Onions are delicious! I broke the world." The blood drained out of his face. "And I did a lot more pranks than those. I, uh . . . I may have some problems bigger than onions."

Mr. Gino walked over. "Hey, Chase, I don't know if you remember, but some scary people in suits are chasing you."

"That's bad," Franchesca said. She held the onion out to Mr. Gino. He shrugged and took a bite.

"*Mmmm!* Delicious! Anyway, I know the perfect place we can hide. They'll never think to look for us there. Not on a Saturday at least."

They all three exchanged glances. "School!" they shouted together.

"I'm coming with," Franchesca said, and she climbed into the back of the car on top of all the boxes.

Chase got in too, and it was only then that he realized he had forgotten his soda. "This is the worst April second ever."

Chapter 12

THEATER CRITICS ARE TOUGH

Mr. Gino pulled up behind the school theater. "Hey, kids, help me with these boxes," he said as he pulled his leather jacket off and threw it on his seat.

Mr. Gino flexed his muscles, and Chase couldn't help but think that the guy's biceps were as big as Chase's legs. Mr. Gino picked up a tiny box and headed for the theater.

"He's not carrying much," Chase said, scowling.

Franchesca picked up a box and started after their teacher. "Aw, what's to complain about? Grab a box and let's get going."

Chase lifted a large box. He struggled with the weight for a moment, started to lose his balance—he couldn't see over the top of it—spun around in a circle, and fell over. He stood up,

studied the box, tried to lift it again, and failed. Then he started pushing the box inside.

As he shoved open the door, Franchesca yanked him behind the main stage curtain. "*Shh*, they got Mr. Gino!"

She pointed through the curtains. Three heavyset men in black suits and sunglasses gathered around the theater teacher. Mr. Gino stepped back and fell into a chair. The men loomed over him. Mr. Gino looked at each of the big men, his face determined and brave. "Are you theater critics?" he asked. "I know there's been some strong feelings about *Get Fit with Santa*, but I'm not going to water down my artistic vision."

"This isn't about that," said Guy Number One.

"Listen, Gino. We're hunting down some illegal activity around here," said Guy Number Two. "And there's a rumor that you—"

"Is this about the package?" Gino blurted.

"Wait a minute," said Guy Number Three. "Now that you mention it, why were there so many Santas in that play? Shouldn't it be just one?"

"Ha!" Mr. Gino shouted. "Only one Santa? You obviously didn't understand my play. Why, when *The Glove Diaries* opens, you'll probably want to know why there are two gloves instead of only one!"

"Hold on here," Guy Number Two said. "Let's get back to this package."

"We don't care about your little plays," Guy Number One growled. "If you have the illegal tech, we need it now. Do you have it?"

"I don't know what you're talking about," Mr. Gino said defiantly. "And even if I knew, I wouldn't tell you." Mr. Gino crossed his arms and stuck out his tongue.

Guy Number One frowned. "Let's give the tough guy some hints," he said.

"All right," said Guy Number Two. "It's ancient. Heavy. And it could fit in the palm of your hand."

Mr. Gino squinted at them. "Are you referring to what I think you are referring to? Why, that has nothing to do with Chase. That's mine! And I'm not handing it over to some government goons."

The Guys exchanged a glance. "Listen, mister. It might be yours, but it's going to cause even more trouble if you don't turn it over to us."

Mr. Gino closed his eyes, and Chase could tell he was thinking hard. Then, after a faint smirk, he let his head fall on his chest and whined dramatically. "I'll never tell you where it is. It's not under the toilet in the men's bathroom in the front lobby though. I can tell you that much."

"Ha!" said Guy Number Two. "He's trying to trick us!"

The three men hurried toward the lobby. As soon as the coast was clear, Chase ran to Mr. Gino.

"Hurry," Mr. Gino said. "They're not very smart or they would have loved *Get Fit with Santa* . . . But they'll still be back soon!" Franchesca helped Mr. Gino up. "Listen, Chase," Mr. Gino said. "There's a package in my jacket. Keep it safe. I think it's what they're after."

Shouts came from the lobby. Angry shouts.

"I'll stall them," Franchesca said.

"Run!" Mr. Gino shouted.

The three men barreled back into the auditorium, just as Chase burst out the side door.

Franchesca jumped in front of them. "Excuse me, gentlemen. May I see your tickets?"

Chase ran to the car. He grabbed the package out of Mr. Gino's jacket and wrestled his bike out of the trunk. He jumped on and did a wheelie. The three suits ran out of the theater. "Try to catch me, slowpokes!" he yelled as he pedaled away.

The three men piled into a big black van. The engine started, and the tires spun so fast that smoke came off them.

"Uh-oh," Chase said, and he pumped harder. Chase sped down a hill. His pedals rotated so fast that he couldn't keep his feet on them.

The van was close behind.

Up ahead, a statue called *The Wave* swirled up from the sidewalk. It looked an awful lot like a ramp. A really dangerous X-Games-level-of-difficulty ramp. But those three guys looked dangerous too.

Chase hit *The Wave* at full speed. His bike climbed the metal statue and flew into the air. He could see the whole town from up here. He could see the clouds and surprised birds flying past him. Way in the distance below, he almost thought he saw his flying spider drone.

Or maybe he didn't fly that high, but that's what it felt like. It was pretty scary.

All the things most important to Chase flashed through his mind: Zoe and her party. His best buddy, Bobby. His mom and dad and Drake. Quesadillas. Baby penguins. He had never had a chance to tell anyone, but he really loved baby penguins.

And just like a baby penguin, Chase couldn't fly.

He was heading toward the ground. Fast.

Chapter 13

BLANK

Chase's bike soared through the air. It hurtled toward the ground like an old satellite returning to Earth's orbit. An old satellite with a screaming middle school student clinging to the back. Chase's whole life flashed before his eyes.

"That's it?" he shouted. "I deserve a longer flashback! I want to liiiiiive!"

The bike slammed into the ground. Chase's body rang like a bell hit by a giant hammer. As the bike pitched to the left, his head bounced off the side of a box truck, and the force knocked him back upright. He wobbled but managed to keep his balance. Chase had never been so thankful to be wearing a helmet. Safety first!

He looked back. Behind him, the black van appeared over the hill. One of the suits hung out the side, shouting at him.

Chase weaved through traffic. Then all at once, he shifted his weight and smashed down his front brakes. The back of his bike spun around, and Chase zipped down a side street, laughing as the van missed the turn. He still had his eyes on the van when he rammed full speed into a black sedan at a stop sign.

Chase flew onto the trunk, rolled up the back glass, and tumbled over the top of the car. As he slid down the windshield, he grabbed the radio antenna to slow his fall. Chase thudded onto the car's hood, his face mushed up against the glass. When he opened his eyes, one of the agents stared at him through the windshield, her sunglasses down on her nose, her eyebrows up to her hairline.

Before Chase could make his escape, she jumped out of the car. A millisecond later, her fingers squeezed his arm like a boa constrictor on its prey.

"We need to talk," she said as the big black van screeched onto the street and stopped in the intersection. "In there," she said and pushed him toward the van.

The other agents pulled open the sliding door, and the woman agent pushed Chase down into a chair and stepped in beside him. The door slammed shut.

"I'm Agent Barb." She pulled out a business card and handed it to Chase.

The card was blank. He flipped it over. Completely blank.

Agent Barb smirked at Chase's confusion. She pointed at the three men. "The big guy there is Guy. Next to him is Guy. And that third guy there, well, that's Franklin."

Franklin crossed his arms. "That's my stage name, actually. I'm an actor in my free time. My real name is Guy."

Agent Barb shook her head. "We've gotta stop putting you all in the same van." She turned to Chase. "We know you turned Fluffy into a lion. We have your fingerprints all over his doghouse."

"Lion house," Franklin said.

Who are these people? Chase wondered. He couldn't help but notice that weird technology covered the walls of the van. Ray guns with radar dishes. A lasso of electrical wire. Masks that looked just like human faces. And a couple of dogcatcher nets. It was a bizarre collection of stuff.

"Look, kid. We're the good Guys," Guy Number Two said. "We're trying to help."

"We got an anonymous tip that the town was going headfirst into a twilight zone," Agent Barb said. "We specialize in dealing with these sorts of issues." She snatched the blank business card from Chase's fingers. "We work for a government agency that investigates weird little events like the ones you've got going on here."

Chase gasped. "You guys are with the CIA?"

"What? No! CIA does overseas stuff," Agent Barb said.

"FBI?"

"No, no, they don't deal with weird stuff."

Chase racked his brain trying to think of another government agency. "The NSA?"

The agents exchanged glances. Guy Number One said, "Look, kid, *we* don't even know what the NSA does."

"Something with outer space, I think," Guy Number Two volunteered.

Agent Barb held up her hands, and the Guys fell silent. "We work with the Bureau of Laboratory Accidents and National Kookiness: BLANK."

"Oh. I never heard of you guys before," Chase said.

"That's because you haven't run into anything quite so . . . kooky before," she explained.

Chase had to admit that was true. Although one time he and Bobby had seen a Sasquatch. But that was in first grade, and they had been in Canada.

Chase didn't feel safe with these agents though. Something didn't seem quite right.

He glanced out the window behind Agent Barb. Across the street, Franchesca crept toward the van. She was sweaty and breathing hard. She motioned for him to stay quiet. Then she pointed at her ears. Chase closed his eyes and listened. What was that sound? It was so familiar. It reminded him of when Coach Buckets made them run "the jaunt" during PE—the sound of feet hitting the pavement. Heavy feet.

Chase smiled.

Agent Barb turned toward the sound. Then she flung the doors open and jumped onto the street.

"Hey, Agent Barb," Chase said. "Is your refrigerator running?"

"I don't know," she said. "I guess I could call home and—"

Just then an enormous refrigerator came barreling toward them. It wore jogging shoes and a sweatband. It didn't even slow down when it came through the intersection but plowed right over Agent Barb and kept running.

The agents shouted at each other.

Guy Number One: "Call it in! Call it in! We have a class-five inanimate object on the loose!"

Guy Number Two: "That's a Form 17b: Living Refrigeration Device with Anthropomorphic Features. Get me one ASAP!"

Franchesca slipped up to the van. She grabbed Chase just as Guy Number Three, also known as Franklin, said, "I hope that thing doesn't have any food in it. Remember what happened in Poughkeepsie?" All three Guys shuddered.

"I still can't eat egg salad sandwiches," Guy Number Two said.

Chase and Franchesca were halfway across the street now. Chase checked on Agent Barb. She was picking herself up from the pavement.

Agent Barb looked toward the Guys. "Boys, we're going to need the anti-appliance weapon. Get it ready."

That didn't sound good. "C'mon," Chase said, and he and Franchesca raced toward Chase's house.

Chapter 14

A MESSAGE FROM THE UNIVERSE

Crunch!

Chase shivered in disgust. "Stop doing that, Franchesca!"

"What?"

"Sneaking up on me and eating caramel onions! Where are you getting these things, anyway?"

"Sorry. They are so delicious I can't help myself! And it seems like everyone is selling them these days."

Yesterday caramel onions had been a new invention, and today they were flying off the shelf at every corner store. What had changed? Had Chase so easily influenced all of Mitchell View to eat something disgusting? Were the people of Southern

California so easily tricked into a new fad? Or was there something more sinister at work? "I wish I knew what was going on," Chase said.

Crunch!

"They're Walla Walla onions, you know," Franchesca said. "They're sweet, like an apple."

Chase didn't buy it.

"Okay," he said. "Let's focus on getting off the street and hiding out somewhere before those agents find us again."

Just then, the black sedan turned onto the street. Chase and Franchesca ducked behind a car and watched it pass. "I think I know what's going on," Franchesca whispered as they continued toward Chase's house.

"Awesome!" Chase whispered back. "What is it?"

She looked him in the eyes. "The universe is teaching you a lesson."

"What?!"

She nodded, and she seemed very certain of herself. "That's it. Just wanted you to know."

The sedan came back the other way. Agent Barb drove slowly, her sunglasses on the tip of her nose, her eyes searching for them. "Quick, behind this fire hydrant," Chase whispered. They huddled down behind it. Agent Barb rolled toward them.

The fire hydrant was not big enough to cover two middle schoolers.

"My grapefruit is after me!" A man across the street ran out of his house.

Agent Barb jumped out of the car and headed that way.

Chase peeked from behind the hydrant.

Agent Barb lifted her hands and said, "Sir, be calm. I'm here to help." But the man ran away down the street. Agent Barb looked at his house, skeptical. Without warning, about six hundred grapefruit and a couple of oranges came rolling out of the front door. They looked mad.

"Who buys that much grapefruit?" Chase wondered.

Agent Barb slid across the sedan's hood, jumped in the driver's seat, and hit the gas. The grapefruits rolled after her. One grapefruit saw Franchesca and Chase and bounced over.

"It doesn't make any sense," the grapefruit said. "And you're going to pay."

Chase felt a sudden urge to hide behind Franchesca. But he fought against his instincts and put himself between the angry citrus and his friend. "What doesn't make sense?"

"You humans call us *grapefruit* when you already have grapes—which are fruit. We're nothing like grapes. So you're going to pay!" The grapefruit bounced toward Chase.

"Run, Franchesca!"

But instead of running she just—*crunch!*—took a big bite of caramel onion.

The grapefruit paused, a look of horror on its face. "You monster," it whispered. "Are you eating fruit?"

"Onions aren't fruit," she said, munching with her mouth full. "But I bet caramel onions go really well with grapefruit for dessert!"

The grapefruit let out a terrified bark and rolled after its friends.

Interesting. The city seemed to be overrun with angry produce. Chase wasn't any closer to understanding what was happening, but he didn't think the universe was trying to punish him. After all, what had he ever done to the universe?

"That grapefruit had a good point," Chase said. "There's only one person I know who will have an answer to this."

Franchesca crossed her arms. "You know someone who has an answer to what's happening?"

"No. I know someone who will know why we call them grapefruits. We need Bobby. He's the smartest person I know."

"Good idea," Franchesca said. "And we're almost to his house."

Chase looked sideways at her. "How do you know where Bobby lives?"

Franchesca blushed. "No reason. I sold Girl Scout cookies door-to-door. Or I like to look at satellite imagery of neighborhoods. Or maybe he mentioned it in class once. Something like that."

Chase narrowed his eyes. She was acting suspicious, but he couldn't put his finger on what was happening. Bobby would know what was going on. Bobby always knew what was going on.

Chapter 15

BOBBY NEEDS A HAND

"I have no idea what is going on," Bobby said. He drummed his fingers against the table in his dining room. Chase and Franchesca had snuck to his house, keeping an eye out for the BLANK sedan that haunted the neighborhood.

"It's got to be related to my pranks," Chase said. "The fruit coming to life, Fluffy the lion, the running refrigerator, the caramel onions. But how?"

The three friends paced the room, crisscrossing around one another. "Also, why are grapefruits even called that?" Chase mused. "It makes no sense."

Bobby marched past Franchesca. "Grapefruits grow clumped together on the tree like giant yellow grapes. That's why."

"Huh," Chase said as he circled the dining table. "That makes sense."

They paced in silence for another few moments. Then Franchesca floated her theory: "It seems to me that the universe is trying to teach Chase a lesson."

"An interesting suggestion," Bobby admitted. "However, fruit coming to life, running refrigerators . . . these things are against the laws of the universe. I don't think the universe would break its own laws just to show up one middle school kid."

There was a knock at the door. Not the front door though— the basement door. The door that led to the secret lair. "Ignore that," Bobby said at once.

"What other pranks did you do?" Franchesca asked as she reached the corner of the room and spun around.

"There was the foam. Decorating the office," Chase said. "The flying spider. The toilet clowns." Chase hesitated. "I told my brother that my parents had disappeared."

"That's dark," Franchesca said.

"That's what I said." Bobby put a hand on her shoulder. "I wish you had been here with me to convince him not to do it."

Franchesca's face went red again, and Chase watched her carefully. Why did she keep blushing? Was she too hot? Did she have some sort of skin pigment malfunction? Was it some kind of sunburn that came and went?

"I wish I had been here with you too," Franchesca said, her voice quiet.

Chase snapped his fingers. Franchesca and Bobby froze and turned to him. "Magic!" Chase said.

"No," Bobby said. "Magic would come with more glittering lights."

They started pacing again.

"Aliens," Franchesca suggested.

"Aliens are too smart to use sentient grapefruit," Chase decided. "If they've seen even one episode of *Chopped*, they know we'd make short work of any fruit they threw at us."

"Technology from the ancient lost city of Atlantis," Bobby said.

"That could be it," Chase said, sitting in the captain's chair at the head of the table.

"We're pretty far inland," Franchesca said. "That sort of thing is more likely at Redondo Beach or somewhere like that."

"Good point." Chase got back up from the chair. They paced. Bobby and Chase knocked into each other, doffed imaginary hats to one another in apology, then paced some more.

"Wait, what was that?" Franchesca asked.

"What?" the boys asked at the same time.

"That thing you did with your hands over your heads."

Chase cleared his throat. "Doffing imaginary hats."

Franchesca stared blankly. "Doff?"

Bobby stood straight and grabbed imaginary lapels on the sides of his imaginary jacket. "To *doff* is to do off an article of clothing. With hats it's a sign of respect."

He and Chase doffed imaginary hats to each other again.

"It's the opposite of *don*," Chase said. "Like when I don my hat." He put the imaginary hat on again.

"Do on. Do off."

Franchesca beamed at Bobby. "Well, I just think it's the cutest thing ever."

"Thanks," Chase said.

There was a knocking at the basement door again. "Ignore it," Bobby said.

More knocking.

"If only we could isolate one of the pranks," Chase said. "Interrogate it."

"Talking fruit, of course," Bobby said.

Franchesca and Chase exchanged a glance. "I don't think that's a good idea," she said. "The fruit are angry. And there's a lot more fruit than people out there."

When the knocking started again, Chase couldn't take it anymore. He strode to the door and put his hand on the handle. "Who is it?"

"Chase, don't!" Bobby shouted as he held up a hand in a "stop" warning signal.

But Chase had already turned the knob.

The door swung open. On the top basement step stood an arm. Well, it wasn't *standing* because it didn't have any legs. It was balanced on the end of the forearm, and the fingers at the top spread out like branches on a treetop. The arm,

96

palm, and fingers were covered with a variety of excellent-looking tools and chargers and doodads. There were even a few doohickeys and whatchamacallits installed—cutting-edge LIMB technology.

Knock, knock. The arm rapped on the open door.

"Who's there?" Chase mumbled automatically.

"It's my arm," Bobby said.

"My arm who?" Chase replied. But the arm had already hopped into the room and was headed for the front door.

"Stop it!" Bobby shouted. "It's been trying to get away all day!"

Chase dived for the arm, but it slipped out of his grasp. Bobby snuck up behind it, but the tiny radar dish on the bicep spun in Bobby's direction, and the arm bounced away from him. It was Franchesca, in the end, who managed to grab hold of it.

As soon as she did, she blushed furiously.

"What is it with you and the blushing?" Chase blurted out.

Franchesca looked at Bobby shyly. "It's just . . . well,

I didn't think Bobby and I would hold hands today. We haven't even been on a date."

Chase's jaw dropped. Now Bobby was blushing too.

It all made sense. Franchesca was flustered at the obviously superior technology of their advanced arm prototype. Of course!

"Quick," Bobby said, starting down the basement steps. "Let's see if we can get it to tell us what's going on."

Chapter 16

FIRSTHAND INFORMATION

They raced down the stairs into the basement lair. Bobby shoved an assortment of tools and tech aside on the workshop table and set up a vise. "Put the arm in here," he said. "And we'll be able to work on it without it getting away."

Franchesca tried to pin the arm in the vise, but it started wrestling her. She gripped the hand and pushed. Franchesca gritted her teeth and groaned as she muscled the arm toward the vise. Bobby stood with his other hand on the vise, ready to twirl it shut on the wild limb.

"I was the state arm-wrestling champion twice, you know," Franchesca said.

"Wow!" Chase said. "The Junior Women Arm Wrestling Champion?!"

She scowled, still pressing on the arm. "No. The All-Comers Over-the-Top Street Rules Arm Wrestling Heavyweight title. I beat out the six-year champion, Gorilla McGurk. I thought he might win, but he weakened in hour three." She looked at Bobby's arm, which was pushing against her with all its might. "I have to say, Bobby, you and I might be evenly matched here."

Now Bobby was blushing. Was it hot in here or something?

"You have to understand," Bobby said. "There's not another arm like this one in the whole world. It will never weaken or tire. It's solar powered, and it has our patent-pending QuadCep technology. That's right . . . Not *bicep*. Not *tricep*. *QuadCep*."

As if the arm had been inspired by Bobby's speech, it started pushing against Franchesca with greater strength. Franchesca struggled, but her arm was losing ground. Then, in a move that Chase would remember for the rest of his life, the arm slammed Franchesca's arm down, spun the wheel of the vise, and trapped her wrist.

The bionic arm leapt from the workspace over to a whiteboard on a wheeled stand. The arm snatched up an eraser and leaned toward the board. "No!" Bobby shouted. "My theorem explaining how to increase summer break by thirty percent is on that board!"

"And I drew a kitty!" Chase shouted.

Chase moved toward the board, but the hand noticed and held the eraser right over his drawing of a cat. Holding his hands up in defeat, Chase backed off.

Bobby tried to calm the arm. "Look, no one's going to hurt you. We're all friends here. Why, think back to all the things that you and I have accomplished together. Just last week you held an ice cream cone so I could eat it. And my legs took you for a walk in the park. Remember, pal?"

The arm wavered, then it scurried up the side of the whiteboard. It flipped the board over to the blank side, threw the eraser to the side, and picked up a marker. Then it quickly, and somewhat shakily, wrote LEFTY in capital letters.

"Lefty," Bobby said. "That mean anything to anyone?"

"There is a famous arm-wrestler," Franchesca answered. "Lefty McGurk."

"You're making these names up," Chase said.

She shrugged. "No. The McGurk family did though. They're deeply committed to arm wrestling."

"It's writing something else," Bobby said.

The arm added something to the whiteboard. Now the message said I M LEFTY.

"It's a code," Bobby said.

"Figures that even your arm would be smarter than me," Chase said.

"But what kind of code?" Franchesca wondered.

If an arm could look frustrated, this arm did. It scribbled again, adding something that looked like a triangle. I Δ M LEFTY.

"Hmmm," Bobby said. "Is that a delta symbol? It's some sort of equation, I think."

"No," Franchesca said. "I believe that's the letter *A*. It's just a little sloppy."

"Someone's name?" Chase wondered. "Is it *Iam*, like Ian?"

"Maybe it's a *one*, not an *i*. Maybe it says 'One a.m. left Y.'" Franchesca looked at them hopefully, but she knew it was gibberish as soon as she said it. They all stared at the whiteboard as the arm hopped up and down, pointing at his writing.

"It's his name," Bobby said at last. "His name is Lefty."

The arm circled Lefty, pointed at Bobby, and drew a smiley face.

"That doesn't make any sense," Chase said. "It's the right arm."

"To be fair," Franchesca said, "everyone's chasing you; you're not chasing them. So your name should be *Chased*, not *Chase*."

"Good point," Chase agreed.

But now the arm was writing something else.

U.

R.

VELCOME.

Chase looked at the message and then at the arm. "Thank you?"

Bobby walked up to the board and inspected the message. "It's a clue."

Franchesca turned the vise handle and freed her arm. "Your arm might be good at wrestling, but it's a terrible speller."

"Lefty is just an arm," Chase said, feeling defensive for the little Frankenstein baby that he and Bobby had brought into the world. "He doesn't even have a brain. Let's see how well you'd spell without a brain."

Lefty snapped his fingers. Then he erased everything and pointed at the board.

"What?" Chase asked. "What do you want, Lefty? It's blank."

All three kids gasped at once.

"Are they here?" Franchesca whispered.

Lefty made a fist and moved it up and down—*yes* in sign language.

Chapter 17

EIGHT REASONS TO RUN

Chase, Bobby, and Franchesca all ran up the basement stairs, just in time to hear the doorbell ring.

Franchesca snuck up to the door and looked out the peephole. "Definitely BLANK," she whispered.

The kids stuck their heads together. "What do we do?" Bobby asked.

"We need a distraction," Chase said.

"We should call the police," Franchesca said.

"How about a plate of freshly baked cookies?" Grandma Agnus asked.

The kids were so startled that they knocked their heads together and fell down. They were rubbing their foreheads and glaring at each other when the doorbell rang again.

"Don't answer that!" Chase said. "It's those government agents."

Grandma Agnus shook her head and headed toward the door. "As if I've never dealt with a government agency. Why, I worked at the DMV for forty-three years!"

Chase had to do something to stop her from answering that door! He jumped up on the couch.

Grandma Agnus stopped to look at him. "Chase, tell me you are not standing on my couch with your dirty sneakers touching my cushions."

He waved his arms over his head. "I didn't know how else to get you to listen! Bobby's bionic arm has come to life."

Grandma nodded wisely. "You told me that yesterday, dear." Just then Lefty came hopping into the room. Grandma looked down at the arm, then gave it a high five. "Who do you think helped me bake these cookies this morning?"

Chase's mouth dropped open. Bobby looked over the top of his glasses at the arm, then looked at it again through the lenses. Franchesca just looked confused and then said, "Maybe this is all another one of Chase's pranks."

"What?! I'm a scientist, not a magician. That thing's actually alive."

The kids stared at each other. The doorbell rang again.

Franchesca rearranged the flower in her hair. "I'll distract BLANK while you two try to get to the bottom of this."

"Thanks, Franchesca. You're the best," Bobby said. Franchesca's cheeks glowed.

The boys high-fived her and ran for the back door. Chase skidded to a stop, turned around, and shouted, "Keep an eye on Lefty for us!"

As Bobby threw open the back door—still looking back at Franchesca—Chase crashed into him. They both tumbled down the steps and onto the back lawn. They picked themselves up, and Bobby looked around quickly. Then he grabbed Chase and dragged him behind Grandma's shed. "I have this creepy feeling someone is watching us," Bobby said.

They peeked around the corner of the shed. Through the back window, they could see the agents entering the house. Grandma offered them cookies. "We should have taken more cookies," Chase moaned. "I hate the idea of those BLANK guys eating them!"

Bobby slid to the grass. "I still feel like someone is watching us. But who? And from where?"

"Aw, stop saying that," Chase said. "We're fine. The real question is where we should go next. We don't have any clues."

"Wrong," Bobby said. "Lefty was trying to tell us something: U. R. Velcome."

"Aw, he's just thankful we created him."

Bobby raised an eyebrow. "Wouldn't he have written 'Thank U,' then?"

Chase snuck another look around the shed. The agents were dipping the cookies in milk. "That's a good point, Bobby. Maybe Lefty's message *is* some sort of clue." Now Franchesca had a trumpet out. It looked like she and Grandma were trying to convince the agents that they needed to watch a show before looking for Bobby and Chase.

"Oh, wait . . . ," Chase said. "I have this too!" He pulled out the package that Mr. Gino had given him. It was still wrapped up.

Bobby took it and turned it over in his hand. "What is it?"

"I don't know. But Mr. Gino seemed to think it's what the BLANK guys were after."

"Hmmm."

"Yeah, hmmm," Chase said back.

"We should open it," Bobby said.

"That's definitely an invasion of privacy." Chase held it up and shook it. "Maybe we can guess what it is from the way it sounds."

He shook it again. "Popcorn?"

Bobby nodded. "Could be. Or a diamond necklace, maybe?"

Chase shook it again. "Look, we have two choices. We open it on our own, or we get Mr. Gino to open it. I know where the theater kids are hanging out these days—some kind of underground lunchroom downtown. Let's go ask him."

"I could just text—" Bobby started. "Uh-oh."

Chase nodded. "Yeah. I left my phone in the house too."

Then Bobby's eyes got really wide.

"My, what big eyes you have," Chase said.

Bobby's eyes just got wider. Then he pointed over Chase's head and said, "Sp . . . sp . . . spuh . . . spuh . . ."

"Spit it out, Bobby! Spaghetti?"

Bobby shook his head.

"Sparkles?"

Bobby shook his head, harder.

"Spam? Spaceport? Spanakopita? *Spectroscope?*"

Bobby took a giant gulp, stepped backward, and yelled, "SPIDER!"

Chase rolled his eyes. "You're the one who told me that at any given moment every human being on earth is within six feet of a spider." He turned around.

The spider was on top of the shed.

The spider was not six feet away, though it was about six feet across.

The spider had eyes the size of softballs and an awful lot of them. Each of its eight hairy legs moved toward the boys.

"Sp . . . sp . . . spuh . . . spuh . . . ," Chase sputtered.

"Uh-huh," Bobby said.

"Run!" they both shouted.

They took off in opposite directions, knocked into each other, and got back up. Then they ran in the same direction and jumped over the fence, making terrified shouts of half words as they went.

The spider watched them go.

Then it followed.

Chapter 18

ON THE TOWN

Chase and Bobby shot through the neighborhood toward a nearby park. "Lots of places to hide in the park," Chase shouted.

The spider landed on a car ahead of them, setting off the alarm. Chase and Bobby screamed in unison, as if they had rehearsed it. They switched directions, jumped a couple of fences, and got on another street, still headed for the park. "This doesn't make any sense," Bobby said.

"I know! How is it so fast?" Chase asked. "Although, we only have four legs, and it has eight. That probably has something to do with it!"

"No," Bobby said, grabbing Chase by the arm before he crossed at a "Do Not Walk" sign. "How can a creature with

an exoskeleton grow to that size unless it lives in the ocean so that the water helps support its weight?" The sign switched to "Walk," and they took off again.

"*That's* what you're worried about?" Chase hollered over his shoulder.

Finally, they made it to the park. Chase scanned the street behind them. No sign of the spider. He and Bobby slipped behind a tree and stopped to catch their breath. But Chase's heart wouldn't stop pounding.

"There's no way that in the current level of atmospheric oxygenation a spider of that size can breathe."

"*I* can't breathe," Chase said. "And we have to find a better hiding place."

"This way," Bobby said. They headed toward the baseball diamond, where some Little League kids were playing a game. The park was full. They passed joggers, dog walkers, and kids in the middle of a water fight with gigantic, gallon-sized water guns.

"It makes no scientific sense," Bobby said. "Which means—"

"We're dreaming," Chase finished.

Bobby shook his head. "It means we're dealing with forces that do not follow the rules of science. There's nothing to keep fruit from coming to life, refrigerators from going jogging, spiders from—"

A shadow fell across them. Chase took a deep breath and then looked up. "Spiders from flying?"

The spider landed next to them, and the boys screamed again. Chase snatched a giant water cannon from a nearby kid and pumped a full gallon of water into the spider's eyes. It scurried backward, blinking rapidly and hissing. Chase threw the water cannon at the spider, and he and Bobby made a run for the baseball diamond.

There was a decent amount of screaming throughout the park. Kids. Dogs. Joggers. It sounded like at least a million cars all hitting the same squeaky brakes at the same time while dogs howled in a hundred neighborhoods.

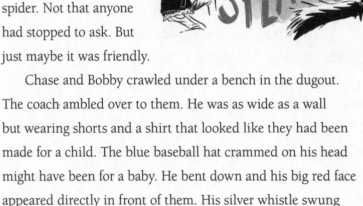

No one likes to find a six-foot-wide spider at the park—even if it's a nice spider. Not that anyone had stopped to ask. But just maybe it was friendly.

Chase and Bobby crawled under a bench in the dugout. The coach ambled over to them. He was as wide as a wall but wearing shorts and a shirt that looked like they had been made for a child. The blue baseball hat crammed on his head might have been for a baby. He bent down and his big red face appeared directly in front of them. His silver whistle swung between them.

"Can you hear them cheering for my team, boys? That's the kind of glory that could be yours!"

"Coach Buckets!" Bobby shouted.

"What are you doing here?" Chase shouted.

"You boys here to join my softball team?" Coach Buckets shouted back. He shouted a lot. He was a coach, after all. He had to make sure his athletes could hear him from across a field while playing a game, all while a marching band paraded around.

"So you haven't seen the spider yet?" Bobby shouted.

"You boys should know I only have eyes for the game. Why, if you hadn't stepped in the dugout, I probably never would have noticed you. If you're not here to join my team, what are you doing?"

"We're hiding from a giant flying spider," Chase said.

"Giant flying what now?" Coach Buckets stood and turned around. His team was in chaos. The spider had landed on the pitcher's mound, and kids everywhere were fleeing. Coach Buckets shook his head. "What is it with kids being scared of bugs? My kindergarten soccer game had to be put on hold because of a single butterfly near the goal. A butterfly! All the kids chasing that little bug and the goal sitting wide open, the soccer ball just lying there like an egg without a hen." He pointed at the boys. "Come on out of there. I'll take care of that spider. I've been training for this my whole life."

Chase and Bobby came out slowly.

"Get back to your positions," Coach Buckets yelled as he ran toward the pitcher's mound. "And you, spider, stay right there. I want to have some words with you! Have you thought about track and field? With legs like that, I could use you on my team!"

Chase turned to Bobby. "Should we make a run for it?"

Bobby nodded enthusiastically. They ran.

A few blocks later they came to a building with a giant window full of strangely costumed mannequins. The theater kids often came to Shakespeare's House of Pantaloons for costumes.

A big bouncer guarded the entry. "This is the place," Bobby said. "Mr. Gino should be here."

Chase looked behind them. No sign of the spider. He approached the door.

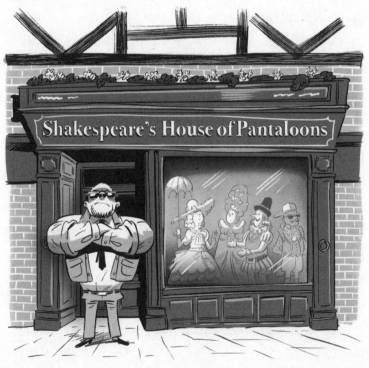

"You can't just waltz in here," the bouncer said. "Especially as waltzing would require a partner for each of you, not to mention the music."

"Uh," Chase said. "We're looking for Mr. Gino. Is he in there?"

The bouncer shrugged. "You can go look for yourself if you can answer a piece of theater trivia."

"I excel at trivia," Bobby said. "From the Latin, a reference to when three (*tri*) roads (*via*) came together and the Roman people would leave notes for each other."

"Whatever. Name a lesser-known Shakespeare play."

"*Titus Andronicus*," Bobby said immediately.

The bouncer nodded. "Good. Now you, other kid. Name a song from the classic Broadway musical *On the Town*."

"Uh." Chase looked to Bobby, who shrugged. He had no idea. "You got me."

"That's correct," the bouncer said, and he stood aside.

As they stepped past the bouncer, the BLANK van came tearing up the street and skidded to a stop. Agents leapt out and headed their way.

Bobby and Chase ducked into the building. "What should we do?" Bobby shouted.

"Hope they don't know their theater trivia!" Chase said as they ran.

Chapter 19

THE UNDERGROUND LUNCHROOM

Chase slid across the lobby floor and slammed his hand into the elevator button. Bobby came running behind him, panting and looking back out the front door. "They're going to get in eventually," Bobby said. "The bouncer is letting them have multiple tries."

Chase pressed the Down button repeatedly. "I assume this underground lunchroom club is, uh, underground?"

"Seems like a fair guess," Bobby agreed.

Chase hopped from foot to foot, desperate to get in the elevator. He heard one of the agents shout, "Lorraine Hansberry, of course!" Then the agents shouldered past the bouncer.

"It's two of the Guys!" Chase shouted, just as the elevator door opened.

He and Bobby squeezed in immediately and hit the Close button. Guy and Guy barreled toward them, leaning so far forward that Chase was surprised they didn't fall over and slide like penguins.

"Hold that door," one Guy shouted as the door started to close.

The other agent hollered, "We just want to—"

The door closed. Bobby and Chase slumped against the walls of the elevator as it descended. "Okay," Chase said. "We find Mr. Gino. We ask him why BLANK is after this package. Then we get out of here. Agreed?"

"Agreed."

With a *ding*, the elevator doors slid open. Chase had been expecting a bunch of theater kids sitting around reading scripts and eating bagged lunches. But it was something more than that. Something much more.

Spotlights in all colors swirled around the room. Upbeat music played, and people danced. There was an entire buffet of food. "Is that a DJ?" Chase asked. "Why haven't we ever been invited to this party?"

"It's a theater party," Bobby said.

"I was a reindeer!"

"You sure were," Zoe said from behind them. "Your invitation must have gotten lost in the interlocker mail system."

"Zoe!"

Zoe took a deep bow and stood up quickly, like an acrobat. She was, as always, wearing a stylish and perfect outfit. "The one and only." She winked at Chase. "Still coming to my party tonight?"

"Of course," Chase said, grinning.

"*If* we haven't been caught by those government agents,"

Bobby said, pointing to the two men in dark suits pushing their way through the crowd.

"Interesting," Zoe said, pleased. "Is this all setting the stage for some elaborate prank for my party tonight? Or . . . did you prank them?" She closed one eye and turned her head sideways, trying to get a different view of the agents. "Are those even actually government agents? Are they actors? Cosplayers?" She grinned. "You two always make things more fun."

"We don't know what's going on," Bobby said.

"No, uh, we pranked them all right," Chase said. "They're actual real-life agents, and we pranked them real good."

Zoe punched him in the arm. "You're so funny." A broad smile came across her face. "And don't you worry—I know how to slow them down. It's almost time, anyway."

Zoe ran to the DJ's station and jumped up behind the mixer. She leaned down to the microphone. "I hope you've all been enjoying the party," she said. "Now it's time for a new thing we're trying after seeing it in the school cafeteria yesterday, thanks to my good friend Chase."

Everyone cheered except Bobby, who frowned and glared at Chase. Chase shrugged. "What? I don't know what she's talking about! Also, did you hear that?! She said I'm her good friend!"

"And," Zoe continued, "we have some guests! And you know the rules about guests!"

The crowd cheered, and a spotlight came up on the two Guys. The agents looked around, confused.

"It's time for Dance Battle Challeeeeeeeennnnnnnnge!" A song with a heavy dance beat thrummed into the room, and everyone around the edges of the room piled onto the dance floor. Zoey grinned at Chase, then leaned into the microphone and shouted, "Now with foam cannons!" As her voice echoed, foam cannons burst to life, spraying down the kids, DJ, buffet, and dance floor.

"Hey, we're not dancers," one of the Guys shouted.

"I may have dabbled with classical ballet," said the other,

and he spun in a pirouette. The crowd cheered.

Zoe grabbed Chase's hand, and his heart beat harder than if he was being chased by a giant flying spider. "This way," she said.

Bobby grumbled, but he followed.

Zoe led them up a narrow staircase with a wide landing and doorway at the top. She yanked at the door, but it didn't budge. She let go of Chase's hand and tried with two hands, but it still wouldn't open.

"They're coming," Bobby said. The agents appeared at the bottom of the stairs.

"The door!" Zoe shouted. Both boys grabbed the handle and pulled.

"Step away from the door," one of the agents yelled. It was locked tight anyway, so they did. And it was a good thing because just then the door flew open and smashed against the wall.

A gigantic blocky form stepped through.

Stately. Rectangular. Tall. The refrigerator.

"Hey, where did it get a leather jacket?" Chase asked. In addition to the sneakers and headband, the fridge now sported a perfectly tailored leather jacket.

The fridge leaned toward Bobby, who reached up and looked at the tag still hanging from the sleeve. "The Whirlpool Big and Tall store."

The refrigerator gave them a slight bow and then turned toward the stairs.

"Uh-oh," Guy Number Two said.

"Run!" Guy Number One said.

But they were too late. The refrigerator boosted itself into the air and did a perfect belly flop. Then it skidded down the stairs like a bobsled on an icy chute. The fridge plowed through the agents, and they cartwheeled through the air like bowling pins.

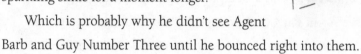

"Let's get out of here," Chase said.

"See you tonight!" Zoe shouted.

"Of course!" Chase shouted. He began running in the other direction, but his face stayed turned toward her sparkling smile for a moment longer.

Which is probably why he didn't see Agent Barb and Guy Number Three until he bounced right into them.

Chapter 20

THE LONG ARM OF THE LAW

Inside the BLANK van, Chase's eyes adjusted to see Agent Barb, examining Lefty. Guy Number Two turned around from the driver's seat, trying to get a better look.

Bobby, Franchesca, and Chase were wedged into a long seat in the back.

"Sorry, guys," Franchesca said. A blinking light shone on her face, then left her in the dark again. "I kept them distracted as long as I could. I did bring these though." She gave them each their phones.

Agent Barb looked them all over,

126

still holding Lefty. "Here's the thing, kids. We're not the bad guys. We're not against you. I'm looking at this prosthetic, and I'm wondering how you kids somehow have access to ARM technology."

"Ahem," Chase said. "That's proprietary LIMB tech."

"Patent pending," Bobby added quickly.

Agent Barb nodded, impressed. "Amazing." She handed the bionic arm to Bobby. Lefty's fingers flexed and wiggled. "Okay, kids, look. It's clear that you've somehow gotten access to some illegal tech. The sort of technology that brings BLANK into town. I know it was probably an accident, but we're going to need you to turn it over."

"I don't know what you're talking about!" Chase said, a little too quickly and a little too loudly.

"Wow, you sound guilty," Franchesca mumbled.

"You really do," Bobby said. He leaned over to see Chase better. "Did you get something illegal to help you ride your bike faster or something?"

"Never!" Chase said in disgust.

"It ain't like that," Guy Number Two said, starting the van. "There's something *wrong* out there."

Chase held his palms out in a calming gesture. "Look, whatever is in that package from Mr. Gino, I'm sure we can all agree that it's his private property and I shouldn't give it to you."

Agent Barb raised an eyebrow. "What are you talking about?"

Chase and Bobby exchanged a panicked look. "Um. Nothing?" Chase said.

Agent Barb narrowed her eyes, and then she moved toward them. All at once, she handcuffed one of Chase's hands to a bar on the side of the van. "Hey! What are you doing?" he yelled.

Then just as swiftly, she handcuffed Bobby to the other side of the van. She looked at Franchesca for a moment. "That's all the cuffs I have, so I'm going to trust you to stick close to your friends."

"Um, I hate to interrupt," Guy Number Three said. "But there's a bug on our van."

Agent Barb sighed and turned toward the front of the car. A *very large* spider pressed its face against the glass, looking inside as if trying to find someone. Its legs

bent to bring its eight donut-sized eyes in line with the agents. All three kids and Guy Number One screamed.

Agent Barb turned back without blinking. "It looks very much like someone is using illegal WF chip technology. My job is to confiscate things like that for the US government."

She reached into her jacket and pulled out a strange-looking gun. It had a spider-web pattern all over the barrel and a dead spider painted on the side. (At least, Chase assumed it was dead. It was flat on its back with eight legs curled over it.). Agent Barb shouted at Guy, "Do you have your anti-spider ray gun with you?"

"Never leave home without it."

"Then let's go." She pointed at Franchesca. "You're going to have to come with us since you're not cuffed." She looked at the boys' handcuffs and grinned. "You two stay right here."

She slid the door open, and the Guys jumped out. Agent Barb followed, dragging Franchesca.

"Is it weird that I'm rooting for the spider?" Bobby asked.

Chase watched them run down the street, shouting and pointing at the spider, which was quickly flying away. "Did you hear what she said?"

"When she called it ARM technology?"

"No! She said WF chip. That's the same thing Mrs. Glorka said about—"

"The Palm Pirate!" they shouted together.

"We've gotta get out of here," Chase said. "If only we could get to the keys."

Lefty rapped his knuckles against the side of the car. A small compartment on his wrist popped open, and a small key fell out.

Bobby grinned and gave Lefty a high five. "Lefty! You pickpocketed Agent Barb!" Lefty dropped the key into Bobby's free hand, opened the van door, and hopped after the retreating agents, Franchesca, and the flying spider.

"Must want to give them a helping hand," Bobby said. "But we've got to get back to your house and see what's going on with the Palm Pirate!"

Chapter 21

A SHOCKING DEVELOPMENT

Chase and Bobby could barely breathe by the time they made it to Chase's house. Along the way, they had kept scanning the sky for spiders and the streets for agents. And they had a close encounter with a monologuing cauliflower.

When they got to Chase's front porch, Bobby sunk into an old rocking chair. "I'll . . . stay . . . here," he said between gulps of air, "and . . . keep watch. You run and grab the Palm Pirate."

"Right!" Chase burst into the house, where his mom and dad and Drake were sitting at the table playing dominos.

"Son!" his dad said. "Where have you been?"

"A foam party and then some government agents kidnapped me!"

"Government agents?" his dad asked, pushing back his

chair and standing up so fast that it clattered to the floor behind him. "Not animal control, I hope!"

"Of course not," Chase shouted back, halfway up the stairs.

"Wait . . . did you say *kidnapped*?" his dad called after him.

Chase threw open his bedroom door. The Palm Pirate vibrated on his desk. It was letting loose all sorts of lights and dings and buzzes and whistles. "So," Chase said, "you *are* up to something."

As he came closer, the Palm Pirate shook harder as more buzzers and alarms sounded from it. Chase grabbed the Palm Pirate and—"Yow!"—a huge crackle of electricity fired into his arm.

Chase flew across the room, hit the wall, and slid to the floor. "Oh, so *that's* how you want to play."

He dug around in his closet until he found his baseball bat—the high-tech aluminum kind. It had been a gift from Uncle Jermayne, but Chase had never seen the point in trying to hit a ball so that no one could catch it. The bat still had a red bow tied around the handle.

He lifted the bat high and swung it as hard as he could down on the Palm Pirate. Electricity shot through Chase and fired him backward again, this time smashing him onto his bed. In his excitement, he had forgotten how well aluminum conducts electricity. Ouch.

"Are you okay, Chase?" Bobby thundered up the stairs. "The whole house just lit up as bright as the opening number in *Get Fit with Santa*!"

"Something freaky is definitely going on with this Palm Pirate. Watch this," Chase said, and he tried to grab the Palm Pirate. It sent him flying into the closet, where an avalanche of clothes fell on top of him.

"You could have just told me. You didn't need to demonstrate," Bobby said. "And look, there's all sorts of information scrolling by on the screen."

They tiptoed up to the Palm Pirate and leaned over to see it without getting electrocuted. "I just saw something about spiders," Bobby said.

"Lion . . . ," Chase read. "Clowns . . ."

"Wait," Bobby said. "Did you put all the pranks on this thing?"

"Yeah. And I just . . ." Chase froze. "That's weird. I just saw a line that said, 'Created by U. R. Velcome.'"

Bobby snapped his fingers. "It's a *name*?! Quick, look it up."

"Right!" Chase zipped out his phone and did a search. "Dr. Ursula Regina Velcome, inventor and reclusive billionaire." He showed Bobby the picture: an older African American woman, with white hair, a slightly crazed smile, and a pair of goggles covering her eyes. She held a pair of bubbling beakers.

"She looks like the kind of scientist who might make monsters in her basement," Chase said.

"That's a hurtful stereotype of scientists," Bobby said.

"But she does, right?"

"She totally does," Bobby agreed.

"Bobby," Chase said, "I have this terrible feeling that somehow the Palm Pirate is making my pranks come true. Think about it. I made googly-eyed fruit, and then there was real living fruit. I made Fluffy look like a lion, and today he is a lion. And what about Mr. Gino's refrigerator?"

"The flying spider too. Chase, this is all your fault!"

Chase swallowed hard. "And it gets worse. What about my other pranks?" He gulped. "Like telling Drake my parents . . ."

Bobby's mouth formed a surprised and terrified O. He paced back and forth in the room, staring at the Palm Pirate. The device was glowing even brighter and shaking so hard that it had moved across the desk. "We have to find Dr. Velcome immediately before—"

"Before my parents disappear!" Chase finished.

Chapter 22

TOILET TERROR

Chase's phone let out a *ding*. He looked away from the berserk Palm Pirate, hoping it was Franchesca. Had she gotten away from the agents? But when he saw the text, Chase's mouth dropped open. "I almost forgot about Zoe's party! And she just asked if I'm still coming!"

Bobby shook his head. "Pull yourself together, man. This isn't Operation Zoe anymore. This is Operation Stop That Palm Pirate."

Chase knew that Bobby was right, but then he remembered the way Zoe's hand fit in his . . .

"We should at least warn everyone at the party," he reasoned. "Just while we figure out where Dr. Velcome lives."

Bobby sighed. "Fine. We can go say happy birthday, but then we gotta get out of there and back to work."

Chase lit up. "Perfect! Let me just fix my look."

"You mean the Prank Attackz look," Bobby mumbled.

"Maybe you should just be yourself." Chase rolled his eyes.

Zoe lived only three streets over, so it wasn't much of a detour. Chase popped his collar and tried out a couple of dance moves. "Ready!" he declared.

They heard the music from the end of the street. It played on an old record player set up by the front door, where Zoe was talking to her sister, Chloe. Chloe looked just like Zoe, except that she was older and taller.

"Chase!" Zoe shouted and gave him a gigantic hug. Chase seized up and stared straight ahead, not sure what to do. Zoe laughed. "Oh, Chase, you joker." She looked at Bobby. "Hey, Bobby!" She waved at him.

"Thanks for coming to my party! Chase, you won't believe it, but I got a Czerweny CZ-1000 from my parents!"

Be cool, Chase reminded himself. "That's terrible," he said as he wrinkled his forehead like he was thinking hard.

Bobby frowned at his friend. "That's an Argentinian computer from the 1980s." He turned to Zoe. "I'd love to see one of those in person."

Chase rolled his eyes. "Dumb. I just like pranks." Zoe had to be pranking him by pretending to be interested in antique tech. He wasn't going to fall for it. Zoe liked pranks, not old computers.

Zoe grabbed him by the arms. "You think the CZ-1000 is dumb? Are you joking? It's the most hilarious computer in history. It has two kilobytes of RAM. *Two*."

Chloe interrupted them. "Look, Zoe, I know I'm supposed to be watching over this party, but we want to go to the movies." She giggled at a guy behind her who was making the entire yard smell like cologne. "If we leave, are your little half-pint friends going to behave themselves?"

"Of course!" Zoe said. "What could happen?"

"That's why you're the best little sister," Chloe said. "And that's why I got you a much better present than an ET-1000 whatever. It's waiting for you in the backyard."

Zoe's eyes sparkled. She grabbed Chase's hand—*twice in one day*—and dragged him toward the backyard. "C'mon guys!"

"Wait," Bobby said. "We have something to tell you first."

Zoe stopped and looked at them expectantly.

"Toilet clowns," Chase said. "Flying spiders. Talking fruit. It's all coming true."

Music—loud music—started coming from the backyard and completely drowned out the scratchy record sounds. "Chase, I don't know what you're talking about, but you're so funny. Let's go see what's happening in the backyard."

She let go of his hand and ran around the house.

Bobby pointed at the front window. "Chase. Did you see a blue light coming from in there?"

But Chase was watching Zoe run off. "I'll be right back," he said.

Bobby took a second skeptical look toward the blue light. He grabbed his phone and started searching for Dr. Velcome's address but couldn't find it. Then he took off after Chase.

In the backyard, there was a gigantic stage with lights shining all around. As they watched, four guys dressed in shiny black tracksuits danced onto the stage. One of them grabbed a microphone and leaned his whole body over it. His frohawk was exactly like Chase's. Chase reached up and gently touched his own hair. He could tell it still looked incredible, just like Zzak's.

A second guy, this one with a fohawk, crooned into the microphone, "I'm Melvin!"

"I'm Mel!" said a third, with his patented dreadlock-hawk.

Then the fourth guy, famous for his curly mohawk, said, "I'm Mello! And we have a special song for a special girl!"

They all four did a simultaneous, complicated bow, then pointed at Zoe. "And that special girl is you, Zoe. Three . . . two . . . one . . ."

It was The Prank Attackz! They started singing their biggest hit, "Girl, You're Special." The kids in the backyard screamed over the music. Zoe stood still, eyes glued on the stage, with her hand over her heart.

Bobby came up beside Chase, and they watched the band prance. "This might be worse than my video." Chase looked at Bobby for confirmation.

"I don't get it," Bobby said. "They're not even singing; they're lip-synching. What fakes."

Chase frowned and looked down at his own black jacket. "Let's go check on that glowing blue light."

They started toward the house. But as they opened the back door, a girl rushed out past them. "The toilet! The toilet!"

"That's not good," Bobby said.

Chase looked into the hall bathroom. A clown's face peeked out of the toilet bowl. It turned toward him and grinned. "What's your name, little boy?" Its voice was friendly enough, but way too high, like it had been breathing helium from a balloon.

"Run!" Chase said.

"That's a funny name," the clown said and laughed far too much. Then a long arm reached out of the bowl as the clown worked its way free from the toilet, growing like an inflating balloon as it came out. A huge halo of red hair surrounded its white face, which featured a big red nose and yellowed teeth. Makeup dripped off its face with the toilet water.

"Run!" Chase said again, and he and Bobby scrambled to get back outside.

Chapter 23

PARTY CLOWNS

The fastest an average human being can run is about twenty-eight miles per hour. A galloping horse can run about fifty-five miles an hour. Chase and Bobby were doing at least eighty. If they had been running any faster, the carpet in Zoe's house would have caught on fire.

Bobby grabbed Chase's arm. "Me and clowns don't mix! Especially wet clowns. Especially wet clowns that come out of toilets! Can we please go and find Dr. Velcome?!"

"Uh-oh," Chase said as they ran out the door.

The Prank Attackz, along with most of the partygoers, were cowering in the gazebo. A giant flying spider hovered over the top.

"Under the stage!" Chase shouted. He did a running, headfirst slide that sent him straight under the platform.

Bobby ran after him, but he had never been good at headfirst slides. As he had explained to Chase, *"This brain is the most important thing I have, and I'm not going to waste it on getting a point in a game."* Before Bobby could join Chase under the stage, one of the clowns grabbed him and lifted him in the air.

"Let me go, you bozo!" Bobby shouted, but the clown just chuckled.

Chase crawled back toward the edge of the stage as he tried to come up with a plan to save Bobby. As he squeezed around a support beam, he saw Zoe running past, right behind the boys from The Prank Attackz. "Zoe!" he shouted. "We have to save Bobby!"

Zoe locked eyes with him. Her round eyes widened, and she glanced from Chase to The Prank Attackz and back again. One of the band members—Melvin—shouted, "C'mon, birthday girl. Our limo isn't going to wait while you save some dumb kid from your school!"

Zoe bit her lip and looked at the clown, who was shaking Bobby like a giant wet noodle. She looked back at Chase one more time, then to The Prank Attackz boys jumping into a limo. "I'm sorry!" she shouted and ran after the band.

Chase crawled from under the stage platform and jumped to his feet. Bobby was his best friend. No one could leave Bobby in mortal danger and be Chase's friend too. "Bobby is not a dumb kid!" he shouted after The Prank Attackz. "He's the smartest kid in our school!"

"He's so floppy," the clown cried, delighted, holding Bobby up with one arm and honking a rubber horn with the other hand.

Chase yanked off his Prank Attackz jacket. He grabbed Mr. Gino's package out of one pocket and put it in his back pocket, then pulled out his glasses and put them on. "I can see clearly now," he said.

Chase hadn't thought of a brilliant plan, but he had to do something. He screamed and ran straight for the clown. Just before he would have collided with the circus freak, he jumped up to tackle it. But the clown just laughed, dropped its horn, and grabbed Chase out of the air.

"I've got two rubber chickens," the clown squealed, and it started to do a clumsy dance of hops and skips.

"What do we do, Bobby?"

Bobby hung limp from the clown's hand. "I don't know!"

"But you've been studying clowns!"

"All I know is that if you want to fight clowns, you have to do something funny!"

Hmmm. Chase thought it over for a moment. Then he shouted, "*Bawk, bawk, bawk.* This chicken has teeth!" and bit the clown in the arm.

The clown dropped Chase and shook its arm in an exaggerated way. "Ow, ow, ow. I'm doing the owie dance!"

"And this one's for Bobby!" Chase said, and stomped on the clown's giant red shoe, which gave out a huge squeak.

The clown dropped Bobby and was now hopping on one foot and cradling its bitten arm. Chase and Bobby hustled together under the stage. Panting, Bobby cleaned sweat off his glasses with his shirt. "Thanks for saving me, Chase."

Chase shook his head. "Bobby, I'm so sorry that I have been completely focused on Zoe. And I'm sorry I've been too busy for you because I've been planning pranks. I just haven't been myself lately."

Bobby grabbed his shoulder. "I understand, buddy. And after what happened in kindergarten, well . . . let's just say I owed you on the prank side of things."

In kindergarten, Bobby had told Chase every day that he was going on vacation to Hawaii. He said that Chase was invited, but they had to keep it a secret. They were going to meet at school in their travel clothes and leave on a specific day. When the day came, Chase showed up in the dead of winter wearing shorts, flip-flops, an aloha shirt, sunglasses, and carrying a sand bucket and shovel. He was completely humiliated. Bobby felt terrible. They made a pact never to prank each other again. The next week Bobby invited Chase to his house and took him down to the basement. His grandma had painted a beautiful beach scene on the wall. They ate Hawaiian pizza and hung out all day. From that day on, they had been best friends.

Chase stared out at Zoe's backyard. The giant spider was rolling something large in webbing. The something kicked a sneaker out of the cocoon. Clowns juggled and did other tricks with kids, chairs, and party streamers. And was that a lion's roar? "I'm going to have to do something," Chase said. "This is all my fault. I can't let our friends get eaten by a spider or get concussions from clown tricks."

"We'll do it together," Bobby said. "And save your parents too."

They gave each other an awesome high five that would have looked really cool if anyone had been looking at them.

Chapter 24

SPECIAL DELIVERY

Chase watched the chaos of the birthday party from underneath the stage. He narrowed his eyes and rubbed his chin. "Right. So here's the plan," he said. "You use that push broom to get rid of the spider. I'll use a plunger to try to get those clowns back in the toilet."

"*Clowns* plural?" Bobby peeked out from underneath the stage. There were at least six clowns now. Bobby shook his head. "Should we save the world or just let it go? Maybe we should just give it to the clowns."

"No," Chase said firmly. "This is my fault, and we're not going to let giant spiders or clowns have the last laugh."

"As long as you're fighting the clowns, I guess. And then we'll find Dr. Velcome."

"Deal," Chase said.

They popped out from under the stage. Bobby ran for the broom, and Chase ran toward the clowns. Chase yelled at the top of his lungs, but he didn't really have a plan. So he wasn't completely surprised when the first clown just scooped him up, grabbed him around the neck, and lifted him off the ground. Again.

But then a familiar car came roaring up the street and crashed through Zoe's fence into the backyard. It was a 1970 Chevy Chevelle SS convertible, lights on and engine growling. A tower of pizza boxes filled the back seat. The driver's door flung open, and there was Mr. Gino with ten pizza boxes balanced on one hand. "Pizza delivery!" he shouted and threw a pizza at the nearest clown.

The clown screamed and made a run for it, but Mr. Gino karate chopped it in the back. "You better run!" Mr. Gino said. Then he pointed at the back seat of his car. "Bobby! Hit 'em in the face with those pies!"

That's when Zoe emerged from the pizza mountain. She aimed a pie at the clown holding Chase and *splat!* The pizza hit the clown in the face, and he fell down, dropping Chase as he somersaulted away across the grass.

"You came back," Chase said.

She threw a large pepperoni and sardine pizza at a passing

clown. "I got about six blocks away with The Prank Attackz and realized I didn't even know them. They were laughing about our town and saying they couldn't wait to get out of here." She looked at Chase with compassion. "They were making fun of how you dressed like them too. And I just thought, well, Chase and Bobby and everyone, they are my friends. That's why I invited them to my party, after all. So I got out of the limo at a red light. I saw Mr. Gino driving by and asked for his help."

"Less talking," Bobby shouted, "and more pie throwing!"

The kids each grabbed a pie and chased after the clowns, who ran as soon as they saw a pizza. Five clowns surrounded Mr. Gino, and he started kicking, punching, and flinging the clowns to the ground. Once he had knocked them all down, he shouted at the kids, "Get in the car!"

The Chevelle peeled out, and Mr. Gino laughed with glee. "You still got that package, Chase?"

"Sure," Chase said and handed it over.

Bobby leaned over to Chase. "Did you make a prank about Mr. Gino being a martial arts guy or something?"

"No. This one was a surprise."

Mr. Gino grinned at them. "In high school, I trained in Clown Fighting. It's a traditional fight style from Italy, invented in response to the Commedia dell'Arte Uprising in 1597. After

many centuries of getting hit in the face, clowns have a deep fear of pies. Including pizza pies."

"Makes sense," Chase said.

"None of this makes sense," Bobby said. And he was right, because just then Mr. Gino pulled his car up in front of Principal Meyer's house. "Oh no," Chase said. "We're busted."

Chapter 25

MR. GINO MAKES EVERYONE UNCOMFORTABLE

Mr. Gino held his hand toward Chase in the back seat. "Where's that package?" The car was idling, and straight in front of them was the one sight you hope to never see unless you've got your arms full of toilet paper rolls: the principal's home address.

"Mr. Gino," Chase said, "you've always been the coolest teacher in the school. You've definitely saved me from my own dumb stuff a few times. And I know I totally deserve it, but please don't turn us over to Principal Meyer. I don't have time for detention. You see, my parents—"

"Give me the package, Chase."

"But Mr. Gino, we really need to go find Dr. Velcome so that we can stop—"

Mr. Gino laughed. "Dr. Velcome? You mean Ursula? Why, she lives just over on Main Street in that giant house that looks like a creepy castle. You know the one?"

Chase and the kids nodded. "Makes sense," Chase said.

"Package," Mr. Gino repeated.

When Chase slapped it into his hand, he grinned and carefully untaped the wrapping. He opened the small box so they could see . . . a gigantic diamond bracelet, shining in the light.

"Wow," Bobby said.

"That looks expensive," Zoe said.

"It's burning my eyes," Chase said.

Mr. Gino threw his door open. "It's a special bracelet I had specially made. You kids stay here for a couple of minutes and hunker down low. My love is a little sensitive about other people knowing about our relationship. But if this is the end of the world, I need her to understand the depths of what I feel for her."

The kids all slid down in their seats as Mr. Gino walked up to the house.

"We can't wait on Mr. Gino. We gotta get out of here," Chase said, sliding behind the steering wheel of the car. "Good thing Mr. Gino left the keys."

"You can't drive!" Zoe said, as the engine roared to life.

"She's right, Chase! You're even terrible at *Mario Kart*."

"Oh no, you guys! Look!" Zoe's eyes were as big as a talking grapefruit.

Principal Meyer appeared at the door. At least they thought it was her. She was wearing jeans and a T-shirt instead of her normal severe suit. She gave Mr. Gino a hug, and he followed her inside.

Bobby choked. "Dude, no way!"

"Mr. Gino and Principal Meyer are a thing?!" Zoe said, gasping.

"Wait a minute," Chase said. "Didn't we prank Principal Meyer last night?"

"Yeah," Bobby said. "We called and asked for the Walls."

As soon as Bobby said that, the walls of Principal Meyer's house faded away. "Oh no!" Chase shouted. "We have to get in there and save them before the roof . . ."

But the roof stayed right where it was, suspended in the air.

Zoe asked, "But how does the roof stay up?"

Mr. Gino and Principal Meyer didn't even notice. Now that the walls were gone, the three kids heard soft music. The two adults stared into each other's eyes and started to slow dance. Chase held on to the frame of the car. He felt sick.

"Nasty," Zoe said.

"Of all the freaky things we've seen today," Chase said, "this is the one I am most upset about."

Bobby glared at Chase. "Did you slip a prank love letter to one of them?"

"No way! I'm a prankster, not a monster."

Now Mr. Gino was down on one knee and showing her the bracelet. She squealed. Now she was leaning in for—

Chase turned the keys in the ignition. "We've got to stop

this bad dream before anyone else gets hurt. Or any more teachers start dating each other."

The car lurched onto the road, and Chase avoided a trash can. "I've played a lot of car video games," he said proudly. He was feeling more confident. "The trick is to drive as fast as you can." He pressed the gas pedal all the way down, and the car burst forward.

Of course that's when the giant flying spider decided to land on their windshield.

Everyone screamed.

Except the spider.

Chase spun the steering wheel hard and drove them straight into a tree. The car (and the spider and the tree) burst into flames. Chase jumped out first and then helped Zoe and Bobby out. "I guess I should wait until I get a license," Chase said.

Zoe looked at the flaming spider, on its back, legs curled up, frying. "That is nasty."

"Not worse than seeing that kiss," Bobby said.

Mr. Gino came barreling out the door, now standing by itself. "What did you do to my car?!"

Just then, a couple of BLANK agents walked down the street. They bent over some sort of machine and studied the readings as they held it toward Principal Meyer's house. One of them turned toward the kids, but his sunglasses prevented them from knowing if he noticed them. Until he pointed their direction.

They didn't look at each other. They didn't think about it. They just ran.

Chapter 26

U. R. VELCOME

U. R. Velcome's house had big towers, the kind
that you would expect to see silhouetted against the full moon,
with bats circling. Beyond the stone fence topped with metal
spikes, sculpted bushes lined the walkway to the front door.
Each one was trimmed to look like an elephant dancing in a
different pose.

Chase rang the doorbell, and the door swung open slowly.

"Ladies first," Bobby said.

Zoe rolled her eyes. "Whatever." She stepped in and—

"Franchesca!"

Franchesca stood there, sipping a drink from a large glass.
Lefty was next to her, waving. "C'mon," she said. "We've been
waiting for you guys forever."

"How did you get here so fast? How did you find it?" Chase asked.

"I just followed Lefty." Franchesca took them down a long, winding stairwell and then through a hall of paintings and lifelike statues. The giant room looked like an art gallery on one end, but as you moved farther along, the room morphed into a scientific laboratory. Bubbling beakers covered long counters, and charts and schematics plastered the walls. But there were two more statues in the laboratory side of the room: one of them was a terrifying figure of a scientist wearing a gas mask, hands held high as if she was about to grab someone.

Chase clutched at Bobby. "I don't like the looks of that."

A voice came from the statue: "Beware, intruders. You have come into the domain of Dr. Velcome!"

"I've seen enough here," Chase said.

"Let's go," Bobby said. "I'm sure the world will get better on its own somehow."

The statue pulled off the gas mask, took a deep breath, and then started laughing. "*Whew!* I had to hold that pose for a long time, *hahahaha!*"

Franchesca smiled. "Dr. Velcome is a bit of a prankster too."

"Come, come, children, I didn't mean to terrify you, just to give you a jolt of adrenaline. Have a seat. Relax. Does anyone want some onion juice?"

"I'll have some more, please!" Franchesca said.

"Uh, no thanks," Chase said. He started to sit on the pedestal of the second statue but paused. Slowly, he patted the foot of the figure. Hard and cold. Then he sat.

"So you found an old Palm Pirate," Dr. Velcome said. "I wondered who was responsible for all the shenanigans today."

"How did you know?" Bobby asked.

"I'm the inventor of the Palm Pirate, of course. You must have found a pre-1997 model. We discontinued the WF chip after '97 *for obvious reasons*."

Chase cleared his throat and leaned back against the leg of the statue behind him. "Excuse me, Doc, but it's never been clear what exactly a WF chip is."

Dr. Velcome coughed suddenly. "Wish Fulfillment chip! I would think that would be obvious."

Chase and Bobby exchanged a look. "I guess that does make sense," Bobby said.

"It's a long story, so I'll tell you the highlights. My brother was, perhaps, the greatest prankster of all time. I enjoy the occasional jumping out of a cabinet to scare someone, sure, but he liked these elaborate hoaxes. And he expected me to use my considerable genius to help him."

"Help him how?" Chase asked.

Ursula nodded, acknowledging the question, and handed Franchesca a frosty mug of onion juice. "He would always say things like, 'Ursula, turn me into a giant robot so I can play in the ocean near Tokyo.' Or 'I'd like to be on the moon wearing a monster suit when Neil Armstrong arrives, Ursula.' Oh, it was all fun and games."

"You could do that?" Bobby asked in disbelief.

Ursula snorted. "Kid's stuff. It was simple, and I didn't mind at first. But it's all he wanted. I got tired of helping him, so I invented the WF chip. All he needed to do was write out a list of the things he needed for his pranks, and the next day those things would materialize. It worked so well that I included it in the next production batch of Palm Pirates."

"Oh," Chase said. "Um. That's not good."

"It gets worse. One day he went back in time to scare Ben Franklin when he was doing his kite and lightning experiment.

My brother was planning to sneak up behind Franklin and grab him while making a sizzling electrical sound like *BZZZZT!* But the lightning struck the Palm Pirate, and *it came to life.*"

Bobby made a what-are-you-talking-about face. "Lightning doesn't bring things to life."

"What are they teaching kids in school today? Don't you know about Frankenstein's monster? Lightning brings things to life all the time! It's the number one way scientists have runaway experiments. Why, just last week I accidentally brought a motor scooter to life. Her name is Teresa."

Zoe crossed her arms and squinted at Dr. Velcome. "If this is all true, where's your brother now?"

"Oh," Dr. Velcome said. "Your friend Chase is leaning up against him right now." Chase jumped up and looked at the sculpture. It did look a little like Dr. Velcome.

"He disguised himself as a statue to scare me . . . but there's one thing he didn't know about the Palm Pirates. When they finish all the pranks in a list, the changes become permanent."

Chase turned to the old lady. "Do you mean to say that if we don't stop the Palm Pirate, Fluffy will be a lion forever? Toilets will always have clowns in them? Fruit will always have eyes? Giant flying spiders will be the norm? My parents will disappear for good?"

"Oh dear," Dr. Velcome said. "You told someone your

parents were going to disappear? Oh dear, oh dear. That was careless, young man."

"But can we stop it?" Chase asked. "You know how to stop it?"

"My dear boy, it's not quite as simple as all that . . . my brother's Palm Pirate realized I was after it. It reprogrammed itself for self-defense." She sighed and moved to the statue of her brother.

"It must be hard for you," Zoe said. "The thought of that Palm Pirate still out there."

"It's true," Dr. Velcome said. "After my brother cemented his own doom, I vowed to destroy them all. But I could never find the one that belonged to him . . . the living Palm Pirate. It is a very intelligent and sneaky foe. And even if we could find it, it defends itself through Extremely Painful Lightning and Electricity. Patent pending."

"Oh yeah, I experienced that already." Chase said.

"Wait a minute," Bobby said. "Does the Palm Pirate get the patent or do you?"

Dr. Velcome didn't seem to hear Bobby. She stroked her chin. "*Hmmm.* With your help, children, I think we have a slim chance to stop this all. A very slim, tiny, unlikely chance that probably won't work."

Chapter 27

ARMED FOR BATTLE

Dr. Velcome paced back and forth between the gallery of statues and her laboratory. Finally, she clapped her hands, and a series of screens came down from the ceiling.

"The Clapper," she said. "One of the greatest inventions in human history."

The screens flickered to life and started showing clips from around town. Toilet clowns ran laughing out of the restrooms at the library. Flying spiders lifted cars parked on Tenth Street into giant spiderwebs that stretched across the alleys. A whole pride of lions played fetch with a tennis ball in the park. People ran screaming from a supermarket, chased by glaring fruit. Principal Meyer opened the door to her office and was swamped by a tidal wave of water and fish.

"Oh no," Chase said. "The pranks are becoming more complex."

"Just like at the party," Bobby said. "There were so many clowns by the time we left."

Dr. Velcome fiddled with buttons on one of the screens, and a new picture appeared: a

BLANK van speeding down the road. "They're headed here, I'm sure. And as you noticed, the Palm Pirate is multiplying its output. This is common before it reaches the final command. When that happens, this"—she waved a hand at the screens—"all becomes permanent."

"What about my parents?" Chase asked.

Dr. Velcome adjusted a knob on another screen until it showed Chase's parents driving their car, with Drake in the back seat. "They're still okay!" Chase shouted.

"Yes," Dr. Velcome said. "Believe it or not, making clowns from nothing is much easier than erasing people from reality. I'm sure the WF chip is working hard to finish that particular task."

"Uh," Bobby looked at each screen. "How come you have cameras all over town?"

"Seems like a major privacy breach," Franchesca said.

Dr. Velcome clucked her tongue. "Please. Your parents all signed waivers when you moved here."

"You said you had a plan," Zoe said gently, getting them back on track.

"Right!" Dr. Velcome crossed to a large wooden and iron trunk, which was wedged beneath the foot of a pirate statue. She yanked it free and flipped it open. As she dug through it, she threw out all sorts of things: scuba gear, a potted plant, a teddy bear, a miniature raft. "If you can get into the Palm Pirate's subroutines and delete the to-do list, it won't have any tasks to complete. If you miss deleting anything, though, that prank will stay true. And of course the Palm Pirate will be trying to stop you the entire time. But with these," she said, holding up a pair of long black rubber gloves, "you should be able to withstand the shocks long enough."

Chase put the gloves on. They went all the way to his shoulders.

"Dr. Velcome's patented No-Shock Work Gloves for Scientists." She waved her hand as if presenting the gloves on a game show. "Why, if not for these, my hair would be sticking out in all directions right now."

"Wait," Bobby said. "Wait just a minute. If the solution is to delete the list, why don't we just give BLANK the Palm Pirate and let them handle it? It's what they do."

Dr. Velcome clucked her tongue. "Unfortunately, only Chase can delete his list. The Palm Pirate will just keep going otherwise."

"How can it tell if it's Chase?" Bobby asked.

"The WF chip is keyed to the wisher," Dr. Velcome said. "Otherwise anyone could just undo any wish. And believe me, the first thing most people do when they see a giant spider is wish it wasn't there."

"So we can't even help him?" Zoe asked. Chase was relieved that she *wanted* to help.

Franchesca shrugged. "He's probably going to need help getting to his house, what with all the spiders and clowns and grapefruit and—who knows, there might even be some grapes or bananas or something out there."

"If Chase is going to get all the way home, he'll need more help than we can give him," Bobby said. He looked up at Dr. Velcome. "Doctor, are you thinking what I'm thinking?"

Dr. Velcome raised her eyebrows. "That the world financial structure is dangerously unstable even without the additional clowns?"

Bobby winced. "Not only that, but also that if we reverse the polarity on Lefty's radar dish, we should be able to broadcast a message asking for everyone to help us."

Lefty pumped his fist in the air and then scurried up to the top of a workbench. Velcome leaned over the arm, and then Bobby and Chase jumped into action.

"Hand me that screwdriver," Bobby said. "No, no, the flathead."

Chase shook his head. "*Counter*clockwise to reverse the polarity, Doctor!"

Franchesca stood on the side, pointing. "What if you took the power cell and flipped it sideways? It would make more room to work."

Zoe cleared her throat. "The subroutine that controls the mini umbrella could be hacked to give cleaner commands to the new transmitter."

Chase paused and looked back at her. That was weird. It was a really good suggestion that required a decent understanding of LIMB tech.

"Finished," Dr. Velcome said, clapping her hands together. The screens rolled into the ceiling. "Oh, whoops. The Clapper again."

They all stood back, and Dr. Velcome handed Chase a microphone. "Every television, radio, cell phone, and computer in town will play your message."

Chase cleared his throat and took a deep breath. Red lights declaring On Air appeared on Lefty's forearm. "Hello, everyone. This is Chase. You might have noticed a few, um, odd happenings today. Those are my fault. I got caught up in trying to impress a girl."

Chase looked at Zoe. He felt his face getting hot. This was *so* embarrassing. Wait a minute—is *that* what had been going on with Franchesca all this time? *Focus*, he commanded himself.

"But I'm not that guy anymore. I'm going to fix this, but I can't do it alone. I need to get to my house, and it's not going to be easy. There are so many things that will try to stop me: government agents, clowns, spiders, lions, fruit." Patriotic music swelled behind his words.

"But I believe that we can overcome these threats if we work together. Mitchell View is a city that has always kept its clowns friendly and its spiders small. I believe we can be that city again! So me and my friends, we're headed to my house. And I hope that if you see us on the way, you will give us a little help: Throw a pie at a clown. Distract a slobbering lion. Give us a friendly wave. And I promise that if I complete my mission, I'll make sure none of your refrigerators are running around town tomorrow."

Chase clicked the radio transmitter off, and Dr. Velcome stopped the music, which she had been playing from her phone. "I'm not so sure about that last sentence, but overall, a good speech."

"How are we going to get to Chase's house?" Zoe asked.

Dr. Velcome smiled. "Don't worry. I have an electric scooter."

She pressed a button, and a giant garage door opened. Inside was a line of weird scientist gear: cars and submarines and giant robots and a rocket. And also an electric scooter.

"Neat," Chase said. "Is that the living one? Teresa?"

"Of course not," Dr. Velcome said. "Teresa is visiting her birthplace at the factory in Toulouse." Dr. Velcome jumped on. "We're running out of time."

"Let's go defeat that Palm Pirate!" Chase shouted.

Outside, sirens wailed louder and louder.

Chapter 28

TRANSPARENT PARENTS

"We can't all ride on that thing!" Zoe shouted over the motor scooter's engine. "There's only one seat."

Dr. Velcome nodded as she put on her helmet. "As my favorite playwright, Eugene Gino, always says, 'More is more.'" She pressed a button, and a seat popped out of each side of the scooter.

The kids all looked at each other. "Bobby and I will go," Chase said. "We started this whole thing; we'll finish it."

"Oh," Dr. Velcome said. "Those always stick." She pressed the button again, and a second set of sidecars popped out. There were five helmets on the seats, and each of them said "Dr. Velcome's Noggin Protector Pro Extreme."

"We could have just taken a car," Bobby said.

But by then the garage door leading outside was open, and the BLANK sirens sounded closer. Chase and Zoe jumped in one side of the scooter, and Bobby and Franchesca jumped in the other. Dr. Velcome revved the engine and tore out onto the street. A pride of lions startled and loped down the street.

"Spiders at twelve o'clock!" Zoe shouted.

"What? It's only 6:15," Chase said.

Dr. Velcome called, "Hold on, kids!" She leaned hard to the right, and the bike spun onto a side street. A terrified bunch of grapes ran out of the street and onto the sidewalk.

"Watch where you're going," one of the grapes shouted.

"You could have squished us," another one whined.

"They seem like seedy types," a third grape griped.

Bobby snorted. "I hate to say this, but maybe Chase should have driven."

Chase stood up in the sidecar. "There's my parents! And Drake!"

Dr. Velcome zipped into the oncoming lane of traffic, dodged a few cars, and pulled in close behind Chase's parents' car.

Franchesca covered her eyes. "I may never get to eat an onion again!"

After a semitruck passed in the other lane, Dr. Velcome revved the engine and pulled alongside the car. Chase's dad rolled down the window. "Well, hello there, son. I thought you were at a party."

His mom said, "We're headed to the hospital!"

"Are you okay, Mom? You're so . . . transparent?!"

"Oh, that's just the flour I put in my hair dryer. It's very stylish. We're going to the hospital because we're slowly disappearing."

His mom waved at him, and Chase could see right through her hand. His dad chuckled. "Don't worry, son, doesn't hurt a bit. Both my legs are see-through now!"

"But . . . but, Dad, how are you controlling the car?"

"I can still turn left and right. I just can't slow down or speed up."

Drake plastered his face against the back window. "Help me, Chase!"

Chase reached over and grabbed hold of the driver's window. "Don't worry, little buddy, I'm coming!"

"It's too dangerous, Chase!" Zoe shouted. But Chase had already jumped through the window. He fell straight through his dad, who was completely see-through now. Chase stomped the brakes and brought the car to a stop.

"Mom and Dad, this is all my fault! Don't disappear!"

"Your fault?" His dad shook his ghostly head. "I thought it was because I was using paint thinner on a project out in the garage today."

His mom was almost gone now. "Chase! If this is really your fault, you are so grooooooouuunndeeeeeeed . . ." She disappeared completely. Only two piles of clothes remained on the car seats.

Drake burst into tears. Chase scrambled into the back seat and wrapped his little brother in his arms. "Don't you worry, buddy, we're going to get them back!" But he didn't feel so sure.

His parents were gone. They were orphans now, completely alone in the world. All because he wanted to do some dumb pranks. He had taken things too far, and he was paying the price.

Chase pulled Drake out of the car, and everyone circled them. Bobby put his arms around the brothers. "Don't worry, pals, you can live with me. We'll be real brothers now."

Chase squeezed Bobby's shoulders. "Thanks, man."

Zoe leaned close. "And you can have my sister to be your big sister. I need a break from her anyway."

"That's really nice of you," Drake said.

Franchesca put the last helmet on Drake. "Look, it's not too late to save your parents. But we have to get to the Palm Pirate *now*."

"Right!" Chase said. He lifted Drake up behind Dr. Velcome and they piled back into the sidecars. "Let's go!"

Dr. Velcome hit the gas, and they sped toward Chase's house. But as they rounded a corner, Dr. Velcome gave a little scream. Then they all screamed! Sixty clowns, maybe more, blocked the street ahead. They had seltzer water and tiny cars and balloon animals and giant plastic hammers. And they did not look like they were planning to move.

"What do we do?" Dr. Velcome shouted. "Try to go around?"

"No time!" Chase shouted back. "We're going to have to go through them!"

Dr. Velcome poured on the speed.

Chapter 29

THE CHASE IS ON

All six people on the motor scooter braced for impact. The clowns smiled, because that's all they could do.

But just then, a small delivery van came tearing around the corner and headed straight toward the circus. A familiar and very cool teacher leaned out the open back door. "Gino's Delivery!" he shouted. "This is my grandpa's van for delivering pizza!"

Principal Meyer leaned out the driver's

window, holding a steaming pizza with a hand sporting a certain diamond bracelet. "I believe these clowns ordered a pepperoni and sardine double cheese *to go*!" She threw the pizza at the clowns, and they scrambled over each other to get away.

Then the sound of hundreds of feet hammered down the street along with a gigantic voice: "What did I tell you? Don't stop running, no matter what!" Coach Buckets burst through the blockade of clowns, followed by thirty giant spiders, all of them wearing sweatbands and running shoes. "Oh, hi everyone! Meet my new track team!"

The clowns were scattering, but there were still about twenty of them ahead of Dr. Velcome's scooter. The scooter was

coming up on the clowns fast when suddenly the Twinz came
out of nowhere. "We heard your radio announcement," Tommy,
or possibly Timmy, shouted. Then the Twinz started pranking
the clowns! One twin pulled on a clown's suspenders and
snapped them back. The other pointed at a clown's shirt, and
when the clown looked down, the twin bopped the clown in
the nose. Then the Twinz started running, and the last of the
clowns chased them, leaving the street clear.

"Wait," Chase said, watching them disappear. "Which twin is the nice one, and which one is the mean one?"

Zoe put her hand on his shoulder. "They're both nice sometimes. And they can both be mean sometimes. Just like me, and just like you. There aren't good twins and evil twins in real life; they're people, you know."

"That makes sense," Chase said.

Dr. Velcome turned the last corner. They could see Chase's house.

And Agent Barb.

She was standing in front of the house, her arms crossed. The Guys were there too, an intimidating and huge wall of muscles and knuckles barricading the walkway up to Chase's front door. Upstairs, in Chase's bedroom, electric sparks were shooting all over the place.

The Palm Pirate was out of control.

The kids all jumped off the motor scooter and ran up to Agent Barb. Everyone else gathered around

them. Coach Buckets and his spider team. Mr. Gino and Principal Meyer. Tommy and Timmy. Even Fluffy showed up!

"I can't let you in," Agent Barb said.

"But my parents have disappeared because of the Palm Pirate!" Chase pleaded.

"All electrical wavelengths indicate there's an active WF chip in there," Agent Barb said. "Once we find it, we'll confiscate it and be on our way."

Bobby and Lefty threw up their arms. "What does BLANK even want with a Palm Pirate that grants wishes, anyway?"

Agent Barb nodded wisely. "We have a warehouse where we keep all this kind of stuff. You know, interdimensional phone books, space slugs, a whole set of dishes from Atlantis."

"Lots of forks," one of the Guys said. "They really liked forks in Atlantis. Strangely, not a lot of cups though."

"We don't have time for this," Chase said. He pulled his friends to the side while the Guys debated how the Atlanteans drank their milk. "We need a distraction," Chase said, "then I'll run into the house and do what needs to be done."

"I got this," Zoe said, and she pushed her way to the front of the crowd. "Stand back, everyone," she shouted. "It's time to get fit with Santa!"

"What?" Agent Barb asked.

"Seems a little kooky to me, boss," Guy Number Two said.

"I don't know, the choreography seems good," said another one of the Guys.

"I love this part!" cheered Mr. Gino.

Franchesca grabbed a caramel onion from somewhere. Chase had no idea where. Was she keeping them in her purse or something? "You ain't seen anything kooky yet," she said, and took a big bite.

"Stop that at once, young lady," Agent Barb said. "BLANK is in charge of keeping kookiness from spreading into the nation, and we will not have people eating onions or doing Christmas-themed workouts in April!"

Chase and Bobby slipped away as the argument heated up and tiptoed inside. But they forgot about the fruit.

"Oh, look who showed up," shouted a banana. "You think you can slip right in here? I see why that would be appealing to you, but there's two of you and a bunch of us."

"Orange you even going to say hello?" asked a tangerine.

"Let's get to the core of the matter," an apple said.

Bobby and Chase stared at the fruit. The fruit stared at them. "I've got two words for you," Bobby said. The fruit fell silent and leaned forward. "*Fruit. Salad.*" The fruit screamed and went rolling and bouncing and flying toward the refrigerator.

"Smart!" Chase said, and they ran up the stairs.

Chapter 30

CHASE VS. THE PALM PIRATE

Chase and Bobby stopped at the closed door to Chase's room. Sparks shot out from under the door. Inside, lights flashed and the Palm Pirate beeped frantically. Chase touched the door handle and felt electricity buzzing through it. He wasn't sure they could get in there.

Chase pulled on Dr. Velcome's patented No-Shock Work Gloves for Scientists. He tipped an imaginary hat toward Bobby. "Well, pal, if this is the end of the line, I just want to say it's been swell being your best friend."

Bobby tipped his imaginary hat back at Chase. "The swellest. Now get in there and save the world, pal."

"Right!"

Chase threw open the door and ran into the room,

184

covering his face against all the energy in the air. He grabbed the Palm Pirate. It immediately let out a huge squeal and pulse of electricity. "They're working, Bobby! With Dr. Velcome's patented No-Shock Work Gloves for Scientists, I don't feel it at all."

Bobby grinned and Lefty gave a thumbs-up. "That's a well-deserved patent, then! You ready for Lefty?"

"Not yet!" Chase pressed buttons on the Palm Pirate, trying to pull up the prank to-do list. It was no use though. The gloves protected him from the Palm Pirate's energy, but they were too big and clunky. It felt like he had layers of bubble wrap around his hands. He couldn't feel his fingers. He couldn't type!

Now everyone from downstairs was gathering around Bobby in the doorway. The flashing lights from the Palm Pirate made their faces glow.

At last, the to-do list flickered onto the screen. There was only one thing left unchecked: "Become the coolest kid in school."

"Oh no," Chase said. "No, no, no!" He looked at Bobby. "It's on the last item. When it finishes . . ." Chase knew what he had to do. "I'm going to need some scissors!"

"Chase! You can't!" Bobby said.

"Scissors, Bobby. And I need them now!"

Bobby slid a tray out of Lefty and pushed a pair of scissors across the desk. Chase pulled off the gloves. They looked ridiculous already, he had to admit. They had at least a negative five cool factor. He took the scissors and cut off the fingers. These would be the goofiest looking gloves of all time. Putting them on would be the same as admitting that he would never be a cool kid. He would never get the girl. He would always be the guy who—well, the guy who was him. The guy who fixed old junk and hung out with Bobby and maybe ran the theater light board. The guy with no fashion sense and—he hated to admit it—he really didn't care. This is what he had to do to save his parents, save his town, and maybe even save the world.

Chase pulled the gloves on and wriggled his fingers through the holes as he turned back toward the Palm Pirate. He looked so ridiculous that he couldn't help but laugh at himself.

"Of course," Mr. Gino said. "Fingerless gloves. That is what my play is missing! That is what my play is about!"

Electricity shot through Chase. The pain was intense! But

he could control his fingers. He pushed through his to-do list, deleting item after item as quickly as he could.

"It's working," Chase said. He deleted the clowns. He deleted the spider. "It's working!"

"Resistance protocol activating!" said a robotic voice from the Palm Pirate.

It crackled and floated up from the desk. Chase grabbed it more firmly. But it was pulling him toward the window!

"No!" Chase shouted. He leaned backward, but the Palm Pirate was too powerful. It dragged him across the floor toward the open window, toward freedom.

Dr. Velcome cupped her hands to her mouth and screamed over the crackling of the Palm Pirate. "It's activating its final defense mode! You can't let it get out of the window!"

With one hand clutching the Palm Pirate, Chase swiped at a trigger on Lefty. "Grappling hook, go!"

The grappling hook shot around the desk's leg as Lefty's hand squeezed around the waistband of Chase's jeans. With the Palm Pirate tugging the grappling line taut toward the window, Chase deleted Fluffy the lion. A gigantic, powerful hum started coming from the machine.

"If there's anything left to delete, Chase, do it now!" Zoe shouted.

Chase deleted "Make my parents disappear." The Palm

Pirate glowed bright white, and he couldn't see the screen clearly anymore. He couldn't tell for sure. But he thought . . . He thought he could still see "Make Zoe fall in love with me."

Chase looked straight at Zoe. "I never even liked pranks! I just pretended because I thought it would make you like me. It's okay if you don't like me or if you never hold my hand again. I don't need a girlfriend. I just want my parents back. I just want to be regular old me. I just want things to go back to the way they were before!"

Zoe shouted something. But there was so much power in the room that he couldn't hear her.

He deleted the line about Zoe. Then he deleted the line about being the coolest kid in school and then—

POP! Squeeeeeeal. BOOOOOOM!

Chase flew into the wall.

Everyone at the door fell backward.

Then Chase couldn't hear any other sound. Or maybe that was because his ears were ringing like a gong. Chase staggered to his feet. Burn marks streaked across the walls. Bobby and Zoe were trying to sit up. Agent Barb staggered in the doorway. But did it work? Had he managed to delete everything in time? Had he saved the world or doomed it?

Chase looked out the window, but he couldn't tell for sure. Would he just have to wait for a clown or lion or spider to happen by? He turned back to Bobby, who was cradling Lefty. "He's not moving," Bobby said.

Chase kneeled down beside him. "Lefty?"

But Lefty didn't stir.

And there was no sign of the Palm Pirate—not even a single burnt piece. It was completely gone.

"What is all this?" someone yelled from the hall. *Mom!* She stepped over the Twinz and Mr. Gino and Franchesca and Coach Buckets and the Guys and Fluffy. As she stepped around Agent Barb, she took a long look at Chase.

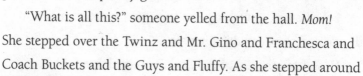

There was smoke rising from his clothes. He couldn't see his hair, but if he had to guess, it was sticking straight up.

"Smoking in your room, Chase? You're grounded!"

Chase ran to his mom and hugged her. "I'm sorry, Mom. It will never happen again!"

His dad stood nearby, arms crossed. Then he held out his gold clippers. "Son, I know this isn't dog hair in my clippers."

Chase smiled awkwardly. "Would you believe . . . lion hair?"

Chapter 31

THE FINGERLESS GLOVES DIARY

Three weeks later, the curtain was about to
go up on Mitchell View Middle School's annual spring show.
It was a new play called *The Fingerless Gloves Diary*, the story
of a young man who saved the world by cutting the fingers off
a pair of Dr. Velcome's patented No-Shock Work Gloves for
Scientists. This show had it all: singing, dancing, government
agents, a weird old lady who sold outdated technology, a genius
scientist, you name it. Mr. Gino had been running obsessive
rehearsals to get everyone ready on time with the new version
of "my masterpiece!"

Chase was running the lights on the ancient light board.
Just like he promised. He rolled up the cuffs of the flannel shirt
he had thrown over a T-shirt and jeans. His fingers had been

burned pretty badly during the Palm Pirate shutdown, but they were healing fast. And the town was pretty much back to normal after BLANK's cleanup job. So Chase was acting like nothing much had happened.

Zoe came back to the light booth and smiled at him. "Hey, Chase."

"Hi, Zoe." Chase wiped a smudge off his glasses with the flannel. "I'm really sorry Mr. Gino didn't let you play yourself in the play."

Zoe shrugged. "He said my portrayal of myself was too stereotypical. But I like getting to play Agent Barb."

"I can't believe she just left for Washington, DC, after everything that happened."

Zoe sat next to him. "I know, but there was nothing kooky here anymore. It's nice that Guy stayed. Er, Franklin. I keep forgetting he wants us to use his stage name."

"He actually is a good dancer," Chase admitted. "And Mr. Gino thinks he has what it takes to go professional."

"TWO MINUTES TO CURTAIN!" Mr. Gino shouted. "TWO MINUTES! Two minutes until the audience recognizes the genius of this production!"

Zoe leaned close to Chase. "I'm glad you're helping out. It's a really fun play. And I know we haven't talked about it, but it was pretty cool what you did. Saving the world and everything."

Chase felt his face get hot. "Well, I kind of put it in danger in the first place."

She winked at him. "Still pretty cool. And I think we should hang out more. Get to know each other better."

"But I don't even like pranks! What would we do?"

Zoe laughed and started walking toward the stage. "I think we're all a little tired of pranks. And I like more than one thing, you know. Remember that old computer I got for my birthday? I love old tech. And I love theater. And it seems like you do too. Why don't you and Bobby and Franchesca come over tomorrow? We'll upgrade some old blenders and make smoothies."

"Cool," Chase said. "I mean, yes," he said. "I mean, right, of course . . ."

Zoe grinned and waved, then ran backstage.

Bobby plunked down next to Chase. He was tapping something into Lefty's keypad. "So," he said. "You did it after all. With Zoe, I mean."

"I guess so," Chase said. "Who would have thought we'd pull it off?"

"Not me," Bobby said. "*Hmmm*, look at this. It seems that there's a subroutine still running on Lefty here. Are you sure you deleted the entire to-do list on the Palm Pirate?"

Chase raised his eyebrows. "It was hard to tell with all that lightning shooting around, but I'm like ninety percent sure. No, ninety-five percent sure," he said. "Hold on, curtain's rising."

Chase hit the lights.

And right in the middle of the stage was a giant refrigerator. It wore a big fake beard and a Santa Claus outfit. And it was pumping its knees in the air one after the other

and thrusting its arms forward—a perfect running-man dance move.

Mr. Gino jumped to his feet and raced toward the stage. "My masterpiece!" he shouted. "Ruined! Get off the stage!"

The fridge turned and ran backstage.

"I might have missed a couple," Chase said, grinning at Bobby.

Lefty gave a thumbs-up.

Chapter 32

END PROGRAM

"**Is it gross** to fix up old blenders?" Bobby asked, sifting through pieces of kitchen appliances in the Technology Graveyard.

Chase straightened from a pile of blender pieces. "I don't think so. We'll wash them."

"And we won't let Franchesca put any onion juice in the smoothies," Bobby said.

Chase shuddered. "Definitely not."

They took a pile of pieces up to Mrs. Glorka's house. She stood on her front porch, squinting at them. "Oh, you two boys. I remember you. Chunk and Bunny."

Chase and Bobby exchanged glances. "Uh, yup, that's us," said Bobby. "How much for this stuff?"

Mrs. Glorka took a look at the pile of blender parts. "A few weeks ago, I heard a pop and a squeal and maybe even a booming noise from that neighborhood over there. You boys know anything about that? Sounded suspiciously like a WF chip teleportation defense module. Are you returning your Palm Pirate?"

Chase shook his head. "We broke our Palm Pirate."

"*Hmmm.* Must be hearing things," the old lady said. "You boys get that stuff for free this time. Frequent-buyer program and all." She closed the door.

"Sweet!" Bobby said. The boys rode their bikes through the mountains of junk toward the gate, brainstorming ingredients for the delicious onion-free smoothies they were going to make with Franchesca and Zoe.

Behind them, a pale-blue light illuminated a pile of rusty waffle irons.

The Palm Pirate's screen was cracked, and the casing was burnt . . . even melted in places. But it was chugging and whirring.

Words typed across its screen.

```
Refrigerator running.
```

Then a check mark appeared beside the words. New words appeared:

```
End Program: Operation Zoe.
```

The processor chugged along for another moment.

```
Load new list?
Loading "Bobby's To-Do List."
"Bobby's To-Do List" loaded.
Hyperintelligent dinosaurs.
```

A check mark appeared.
From under the Palm
Pirate and waffle irons, a tiny
dinosaur crawled out. It wore
a tiny lab coat. The dinosaur
took out the Palm Pirate's
stylus and wrote on the
screen. It nodded once. Then
it picked up the Palm Pirate
and scurried away.

THE END . . . for now!

ACKNOWLEDGMENTS

This was fun! I would like to thank God first! He downloaded this fun idea in my mind and put some amazing people in my life to make it happen.

A big thank-you to these amazing people:

Thank you to my beautiful and smart wife, Asia, for her encouragement and for listening to me talk about the wacky adventure and action scenes in this book. Your support is amazing, and I love your positive feedback!

Thank you, kids! All four of you: Wisdom, Honor, Allure, and Lyric. All of you have witnessed Dad get into character while reading books to you. Let this story be a reminder to always keep your joy and be happy being you!

Thanks, Mom and Dad, for making me read a book each week and then give a book report presentation in front of you in the family room. All those books sparked and fueled my imagination.

Thank you, Matt Mikalatos. It was so awesome working with you! I love that you understand my comedy and added some sauce to this fun fantasy world.

Thank you, Santy Gutiérrez, for making all the characters come alive. The art is amazing! I couldn't wait to see the running refrigerator, and it was everything I imagined. You are awesome! And the cover art is so cool!

Big thank-you to the Tommy Nelson team: Danielle Peterson, Tiffany Forrester, and my amazing editor, Laura Helweg. You all rock, and there are so many more people at Tommy Nelson that contributed to this book in ways big and small. I am grateful for you all and thankful for the love you put in this book. I'm happy to be a part of the Tommy Nelson family!

Thank you to my team!! You always assemble like the Avengers for me! Thank you, Brandi Bowles, Alex Goodman, Mark Temple, and the whole UTA and Levity teams. I appreciate you all!

Thank you to my cousin, Darlwin Carlisle. You are an inspiration. Thank you for being so positive and having courage at such a young age after having a double amputation. Thank you for letting nothing hold you back and having no limitations— just like Bobby.

Thank you to all the creators of the '80s and early '90s movies I watched, which contributed to my love for adventure in storytelling. *Prank Day* has the same fun vibes.

Thank you to all my family and friends. And thank you to you—the reader!—for coming on this journey with me and Chase!

Love you all.

God bless,

KEL

ABOUT THE AUTHOR

Kel Mitchell is a two-time Emmy Award–nominated actor, producer, comedian, and youth pastor hailing from Chicago, Illinois. From 2019 to 2020, Mitchell executive produced and appeared in the new iteration of the beloved Nickelodeon series *All That*, bringing him full circle to the original award-winning show that was his big break. *All That* was Nickelodeon's longest-running live-action series, with 171 episodes across ten seasons from 1994 to 2005. The franchise paved the way for a number of successful spin-offs, including *Kenan & Kel*, *The Amanda Show*, *The Nick Cannon Show*, and the feature-length film *Good Burger*, all of which cemented Mitchell's impact on pop culture. Additionally, Mitchell hosts the heartwarming TV series *Tails of Valor*, which looks at true stories of service animals working to change people's lives, and the educational program *Best Friends Furever*, which reveals the true stories of dogs who are best pals not only with humans but with a variety of different animal species. Both shows air on CBS Saturday mornings. He also recently starred as Double G, an impulsive and unpredictable billionaire rapper, on *Game Shakers* and served as a co-host on MTV's *Deliciousness*, a spin-off of *Ridiculousness* that showcases various funny food-themed videos from the Internet. As a youth pastor, Mitchell speaks to youth on a weekly basis across the country, encouraging them to love God and follow their dreams. Mitchell is also the spokesperson for The National College Resources Foundation, which provides scholarships for students to attend HBCUs throughout the year.

PRAISE FOR *PRANK DAY*

"Kel Mitchell has made us laugh for decades, and this time, he is doing it with stories to share with your kids. I love the mixture of good values with good laughs and great storytelling. Thank you, Kel, for adding to our family library!"

Mayim Bialik, actress and author of *Girling Up* and *Boying Up*

"Fun, fun, fun!!! I love the characters, the pranks, and the overall message of Kel Mitchell's *Prank Day*. My daughter and I laughed and enjoyed the illustrations. This book is clever, witty, and smart. A must buy."

GloZell Green, influencer, entertainer, and author of *Is you okay?*